D1112549

L. M. Beattie
1964

THE GRAVE-MAKER'S HOUSE

The Grave-maker's House

By RUBIN WEBER

HARPER & ROW, PUBLISHERS

New York, Evanston, and London

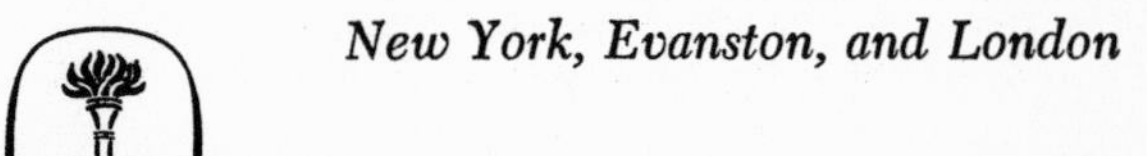

To

Mary Cady Rubinstein

Margaret Farrer Weaver

"Dirge Without Music," on page 38, is from *The Buck in the Snow and Other Poems* by Edna St. Vincent Millay. Copyright 1928 by Edna St. Vincent Millay, renewed 1956 by Norma Millay Ellis. (Harper & Brothers, 1928.) Reprinted by permission of Norma Millay Ellis.

FIRST EDITION

LIBRARY OF CONGRESS CATALOG CARD NUMBER: 64-14388

E-O

THE GRAVE-MAKER'S HOUSE

1

The rear door of the church was ajar to the night. Phares stepped inside, closed and locked the door. He felt his way down the steps, through the blackness, past the furnace. He pushed open the door of his basement room. "Suzy?" he said.

The cot rustled in the blackness.

"Yes, Phares."

Phares felt his way to the cot and sat on the edge. In the darkness, he touched soft flesh.

"Wait, Phares," Suzie said.

"We will not," Phares whispered. "We chust will not."

Later, Suzie said, "Shall I light the light, Phares?"

"No."

She squeezed his arm. "You make the whole church shake."

Phares corded his arm into muscle under her hand. "You help, Suzie. I could not do it alone."

Suzie laughed. She rose and moved through the dark room. "Did you have a good day, Phares?"

"A lot happened," Phares said.

2

She sat beside him, buttoning her blouse. "What did you do?"

"For one thing I went to the Black Dragon Auction."

"Did you buy something?"

"Some grass seed and a quart of honey. I wanted a shovel, but the cheapest one brought two dollars."

"You didn't get in any fight again, did you?"

Phares snorted. "No, they learned already to leave me alone."

"You're a good man," Suzie said. "You know that, Phares?"

Phares was silent.

"When can we get married?" Suzie said.

"We can't," Phares said. "We chust can't get married until we have a place to live."

"How long yet will that be?"

"Soon."

"You keep saying that."

"Jonas cannot live forever," Phares said.

"But he does," Suzie said. "It's forever already. You do the sexton work now; you should have some say. Did you talk to him about a housekeeper?"

"Ach, he won't hear to that. Anyhow, we couldn't live like man and wife that way."

"What keeps him alive, Phares? He's old; he had already a heart attack. I saw him today and he looks stronger again."

"It won't be so long," Phares said.

"It will if you just wait and never do nothing."

"Did it rain here today, Suzie?"

"There was a gust about three; it rained pretty hard," Suzie said.

"I was on my way home from the Black Dragon," Phares said. "I got caught in it. I stopped off in Becker's woods." A cricket chirped in the corner.

"And you saw the Goat Woman," Suzie said. "I wish you'd stay away from that old hex."

"She said it out today; she said I would get it."

"She's just leading you on, Phares. You listen to me."

"No," Phares said. "She knows things—"

"What did she say this time that's so new?"

"She has a lot of different seeds, and she puts them out in saucers, and she studied them and she said, 'Phares, you will get a house.' "

"Huh! Yes, you'll get a house, but when?"

"She sifted the seeds and she said she saw a grave opening up."

"She knows you're the sexton now, Phares. She knows you dig graves."

"She said she saw the acorns sprouting; she said my house would have oak rafters. I looked, Suzie; the rafters are oak."

"Huh," Suzie snorted again. "You want a house—hold a pillow over his mouth. It wouldn't take three minutes."

"If he'd make me mad, I would do it."

"Yes, that's just your trouble, Phares. Everybody knows your temper. That would be the worst thing—to do it when you're mad."

Phares put his arm over Suzie's shoulder.

"It's too bad we have to sit in the dark like this," Suzie said.

"You know, Suzie," Phares said, "we're not the only ones that meet on the sly."

"No, I guess not," Suzie said.

"When you work for Doc Evans; when you clean house back there, does he ever try anything with you?"

Suzie looked at Phares. "No, Phares. You know I wouldn't let him."

"When I cut across Zimmerman's Hill this afternoon, I saw his car parked in the woods."

"I guess he has a right," Suzie said. "He has a lot there; he's gonna build a house."

"He wasn't alone."

"Oh," said Suzie. "Did you see who it was?"

"It was his nurse—the Franck girl from Earltown."

4

Suzie moved closer under his arm. "Well," she said. "We didn't invent it. Did they see *you?*"

"Yes, ha, there was excitement. She screamed. He jumped out of the car."

"Doc didn't threaten you, did he?"

His hand tightened on her shoulder. "Who's got the nerve?" he said.

Suzie stood. "If you think just because other people meet on the sly, I'm gonna meet you here in the church basement forever, you got another think comin'."

"All right, Suzie," Phares said.

She reached up, pulled his bearded face down and kissed him. "You want me, don't you?"

"Yes."

"Then do something."

"What about Kenneth?"

"Make sure he's asleep. Phares, don't worry about the boy. He's afraid of you."

"It's what the Goat Woman said."

"That old Powwow again," Suzie said. "What did she say?"

"I don't understand such things so good," Phares said. "But she had some seeds in one saucer—nightshade seeds, she said they were, and she said they were turning on me."

"So?"

"And I said chust what you said, 'So?' and then she acted like she didn't wanta talk, and I hit the table with my fist till the seeds flew every which way. . . ."

Suzie laughed. "That's you."

"And she mumbled something that my seed would turn against me, and I asked her what she meant and she wouldn't say."

"Phares," Suzie said. "I told you before; you put too much stock in ghost stories and fortune-tellers. You listen to me and you won't have to worry about the boy or the Goat Woman." She pressed against him. "You know, Phares, you fool around and Jonas might leave the house to the church. Reverend Richter would like that."

"You wait, Suzie," Phares said.

She squeezed his hand. "I trust you, Phares." She kissed him. "I have to go." The door closed behind her. Her heels clicked through the furnace room.

Phares stood alone in the church. He walked into the next room and struck a match. Hot-air pipes from the furnace clung like a huge spider to the ceiling. He went up into the church-yard. The moon was draped by black clouds; the only sound was the crying of crickets.

2

Galen Herr scanned his roll book and closed it. All present. He got up from the desk and looked at his class. The students—all twelve of them, his junior English class—smiled. Anticipation was in their faces. The last class of the day and the day was Friday.

"Well," said Mr. Herr, "I have a treat for you. During the next few days we are going to read a fascinating play. I know that you will like it, that you will read it with intense interest and come to class every day bursting with enthusiasm to discuss it." He smiled, and the class groaned.

He carried the anthology from the desk to the south window that looked out over the valley of the Crooked Creek. He pushed the window up and sat on the sill, his foot dangling.

"This play," he said, looking through the window, "was written by an Englishman. Who do you think it was?"

"Shakespeare," the class said.

"That's right," said Galen Herr. "William Shakespeare. You read *The Merchant of Venice* last year, and in the ninth grade you read *Julius Caesar*, and you'll read *Hamlet* next year. But this one I like best of all— Well, now, Jake Sauder still has his tobacco out. Katherine, why hasn't your father put away his tobacco yet?"

"It's not his fault," Katherine Sauder said. "His hemoroads are acting up. I heard him tell Mom he has to grease them every two hours, and he ain't—isn't supposed to do nothing for another two days."

Mr. Herr looked at the class; only Kenneth Zercher blushed a little to reveal that he knew about hemorrhoids.

"He isn't supposed to do *anything,*" Mr. Herr said. "Well, Katherine, tell your father I'll help him put away tobacco after school next week. One of these days there'll be a frost." He swung his leg off the window sill and pulled the window down. He walked slowly toward the back of the room, where the window showed the cemetery and the backs of the houses on the south side of Main Street. A bank of clouds was forming in the west.

"What Shakespeare play is in this book?" Two hands went up. "Kenneth."

"*Macbeth,*" said Kenneth Zercher, turning in his seat. Kenneth smiled, and an indentation appeared in his cheek. His black hair was rumpled. "I read it the other night."

"Good," the teacher said. "You'll enjoy it again. Has anyone else read it?"

No one had.

"If you like murder," Galen said, "you'll have your fill in this play. If you believe in ghosts, you'll meet a few—" He lowered the book. "You all believe in ghosts, don't you?"

"Oh, we know there aren't any," Gertrude Schaeffer said.

Crist Bixler raised his hand. "I heard Eevich Yegar. I heard him myself. My mom got me up at night to hear him. I heard the horse's hoofs and I heard the hounds bark, just as plain. They went just below the ridge and down across Levi Martin's pasture. It was moonlight and you couldn't see a thing, and

Mom told me the story about Eevich Yegar, and I heard him with my own ears."

Hands waved. "Kenneth," Mr. Herr said.

"My father tells how one night he was coming home from Five Points, and right at the bottom of the camp-meeting hill a big wolflike dog with fiery eyes came out of the woods and jumped on his back. My father couldn't shake him off. The dog didn't bite or anything, just hung on his back. You know how strong my father is. Well, he said the dog was heavier than anything he ever lifted before, and he staggered the whole way to the top of the camp-meeting hill. The revival tent was up and my father managed to get to it and the dog disappeared—just like that—" Kenneth snapped his fingers. "He looked around for it, but it was gone."

"And—so you believe in ghosts too?"

"I guess I believe in *that* one. If you heard my father tell it, you'd believe it too."

"You folks ought to enjoy this play then," the teacher said. He raised the book. "In addition to ghosts, we have witches—witches to make your hair quiver. And some of you like poetry." He put the book down again. "There's lots of that. Beautiful language—words strung together like jewels."

"Gee," said Florence Weber.

"Mr. Herr." Crist Bixler was waving his hand. "How many murders are there in this play?"

"Oh, I don't know," Galen said, "five at least. There's plenty of blood, I can tell you. Blood all over the place."

The boys grinned and the girls grimaced.

"Why is it," Crist said, "that you don't let us read comic books? They don't have *that* much blood and you say *they're* too violent?"

The class waited.

"That's a good question, and I'll try to show you as we read. In the comic books the violence is there just to shock us or to excite us, but in Shakespeare the violence is there to teach us about people. Shakespeare is concerned with the forces of good and forces of evil at work in people's lives all the time. That's why we read him." Mr. Herr's face was serious. "Maybe we can learn to recognize the evil in our own lives, the good and the bad mixed up in Fair Hill, in this school, in our homes. Do you see what I mean?"

His students looked at him.

"That's what we call applying literature to life." Mr. Herr walked to the blackboard. "That's how we learn our duty, our responsibility." He chalked a house on the board. "You see," he said, "our life is like a structure of pleasure on a foundation of responsibility."

Students frowned.

"What I mean is this—we should enjoy life as much as we want to so long as the lives of the people around us—and I mean right around us—are not threatened. We should enjoy life as much as we can—hunt, fish, play tennis, golf, watch baseball, play with the kids, work, love, eat, sleep—whenever we have the chance. But we must accept this joy, not as a right, but as good fortune, and be ready on a minute's notice to give it up if the life around us becomes evil. When people around us—close to us—are blighted or threatened, we set aside our own search for pleasure and set things straight. Do you understand?"

Some students nodded.

Galen Herr put the chalk down and walked back to the window. The thunderstorm was coming in over Zimmerman's Hill.

"All right, let's read."

3

Phares stood inside the doorway and glared at Kenneth and Jonas. Jonas was lighting the coal-oil stove and Kenneth was trying to open a can.

The siren on top of the fire hall a half block up the street wailed its Saturday noon signal. Phares waited until the two blasts were finished.

"I'm hungry. Why ain't dinner ready?"

"It'll be ready soon," said Kenneth, looking at the can.

"I work like a goddam dog," said Phares. "I come over to eat so I can get back to work—and *Gut fadumpsi* I have to wait. While other people walk all morning." He tore open the loaf on the table and slid a knife into the dish of light molasses.

He hit the table, making all the dishes jump. "*Gut fadumpsi noch a mol.* Don't bring that sugar water for me—I bought honey yesterday. Put it on the table." Kenneth fumbled with the can. Jonas sighed and rubbed his forehead with a thin hand.

"It's too bad, Phares, that you carry on so. I know you work hard. I'll be stronger in a little while; I'm feeling better every day. I'll be able to help again soon."

Phares sat heavily into the chair.

Kenneth ladled out tomato soup and sat down with the other two.

"Ach, it's not the work," said Phares. "I can work." He clenched his teeth and his beard twitched.

"Then what is it?" Jonas said, softly.

Phares sucked a spoonful of soup. Jonas looked at him. Kenneth spread butter.

"Then what is it, Phares?" Jonas said.

Phares slammed the spoon down in the soup. A chip flew from the rim of the plate and the liquid splashed over the table, in the molasses and on Jonas' white shirt in a red splotch. Why were they so stupid? Didn't they know what a man needed? How could he answer a stupid question like that? How could he say that he wanted to have a house and a wife, that he wanted to walk up to Kutz's store and have people smile at him?

"What is it that makes you so mad all the time?" Jonas' voice was muffled. "You tramp on the ground as if you want to break it. When you dig a grave, you do it so mean like, as if you're in a hurry to get the body in it."

"I can throw out a grave faster than anybody in the world. There I give you right," Phares said.

"Yes, well, maybe you oughta do it slow sometime." Jonas looked up and his voice became stronger. "Maybe if you dug a grave slowly and picked out the big stones and took some time to break up the big clots of earth—you know, like you were preparing a place for someone to rest. Maybe this would be better."

Phares made a noise. "Ach, you talk foolish. Kenneth, soup!" Kenneth jumped up and filled his father's plate. Phares ate noisily, tilting the plate to get the last spoonful, wiping out the bottom with a piece of bread. "Chust like a foolish old man." He sucked his teeth. "Those caskets are lined with silk; Charlie Buch lays them in there on a pile of pillows a foot thick. Pick out the big stones—why you talk dumber than that fake Christer, Reverend Richter."

Jonas lowered his head almost to the table top. "Yes, well," he said, quietly. "Some people a body just can't talk to; all they hear is the words. I just meant if you dug a grave right, it might help you."

Phares was nodding his head before Jonas finished. "I know, I hear Richter talk like that. I hear him still on Sundays when he's up there shootin' off his big mouth and I'm down in my room; love your neighbor as yourself. You take that all, don't you?"

Jonas' eyes glowed. "You *hate* your neighbor. The way you hate yourself. I guess that's just the whole trouble. You can call Reverend Richter what you want to and it won't help that: to have the Devil on your back the way you do."

Phares held his breath.

Jonas raised his voice, "I just said to Kenneth this morning down at Stauffer's Dam—"

Phares slammed both fists against the table top and jumped up.

"Oh, you chust said to Kenneth this morning." He pointed a finger. "You find something else to do besides walk around and turn a boy against his father."

"Father, he wasn't," Kenneth said.

"You shut up."

Jonas got up and held his hands out toward Phares. "Phares, Phares, Phares, this won't do. We can't go like this."

Phares took the frail arms and forced Jonas back into the seat. "You're damn right we can't!" he said. "I'm going to have some say now about how things will go. I'm going to have a housekeeper come here for one thing to do the woman's work. I will have more than soup and sugar water."

Jonas rose again. "A housekeeper, come here—live here—that's what you—" He shook his head. "In front of the boy?"

Phares seized Jonas by the shoulders. "I do the work here now. I can decide."

Kenneth leaped between them and tugged at his father's arms.

"Please, Father, please, don't. Please let Jonas be."

With the back of his hand, Phares slapped the boy into the range.

"This is my house," Jonas wheezed. "You will not bring Suzie Kulp into this house to live. She has a bad name."

Phares lifted the old man. "A bad name!" he said. "A bad name!" The old man's head snapped back and forth.

The old man gasped and tried to pull free.

"A bad name!" Phares said. He held Jonas up, shaking him.

Kenneth tore at his father's shirt. "Please!" he screamed. "Please!"

The old man's head rolled back and forth. His shoes were free of the floor.

Phares roared and swung the old man against the boy. Kenneth struck the door, opened it, ran through the hall and into the street. He looked wildly about.

Across the street Chet Lehman was stretching a chamois over his car fender to dry. He dropped the sponge into the bucket.

Kenneth, white-faced and breathless, ran up.

"Ken, what is it? What's the hurry?" Chet asked.

The boy moved his mouth. No words came. Then suddenly, "Come quick, Mr. Lehman, Father's shaking Jonas."

Chet looked at the little cottage across the street.

"What, Kenneth?"

"I'm afraid Father is going to hurt Uncle Jonas; he's so mad."

Chet shifted his weight from one foot to another, touched the elastic bands on his shirt sleeves. "Ach, Kenneth, it can't be. You're excited." He began to loop the hose.

Kenneth whispered, "Please, you must." He turned and ran back across the street into the house.

Phares was coming from the downstairs bedroom, just closing the door.

His manner was calm. He walked slowly toward the stove, then turned toward Kenneth.

"Where's Jonas?" the boy said. "Where is he?"

"He's had a spell," Phares said. "I put him in on the bed."

Kenneth started toward the door. Phares stepped in his path.

Kenneth stopped. "I'm going for Doc Evans."

The father held the boy's shoulder. "Wait," Phares said. "Where did you go chust now?"

"I went to Chet Lehman."

"What did you say to him?" The hands pressed the boy's shoulder.

"I–I said to come over–something happened to Jonas," the boy said.

Phares's fingers tightened. A faint knocking sound came from the kitchen door. Phares stiffened and looked at Kenneth.

"Where did you say you went?"

"To Chet Lehman," said Kenneth, trembling.

"And what did you say to him?"

"I–I said, 'Mr. Lehman, come over; something happened to Jonas.' "

Phares stood still. The knocking stopped. Kenneth sagged to his knees, sliding from under Phares's hands.

"*Was?*" Phares said.

The knocking began again.

"I don't know!" Kenneth said. ". . . I don't know . . . I can't. . . ."

The knocking was quiet and dogged.

Phares leaned over and grabbed Kenneth's shoulder and swung him to his feet.

"You shut up!" he said, and went toward the door.

Kenneth held his hands against his face, his mouth twisting. His cheeks were hot and dry.

Phares opened the door.

Chet Lehman stood in the doorway.

"What do you want?" Phares said.

"Ah, is there any trouble? Is there everything all right—I thought Jonas—?"

"Jonas had a little spell again," said Phares. "A little like the one he had awhile back."

"Can I do something, maybe? The boy said . . ."

"What?" Phares said. "The boy said what?"

Chet stepped back. "Jonas . . . Jonas was sick . . . or something. Had a spell."

"Yes," Phares said. "Kenneth is going to fetch the doctor. Go, Kenneth."

The boy brushed past Chet and broke into a run up the main street of Fair Hill. "Let Nellie and I know if we can help," Chet said. "Nellie has a pie for Jonas again."

"There's nothing you can do; chust mind your own business."

Phares closed the door. He stood. Then he went over to the dish bench, poured some water from the teakettle into the basin, added some cold water from the bucket, and reached for the soap.

4

Clinton Evans, M.D., pulled his new Oldsmobile into the driveway, stepped out, and looked at the rear end of his car. It stuck out over the sidewalk. Mildred had parked the Cadillac too close to the sidewalk again.

"Damn it," he thought. "Why must she always park as if she lived here alone?" He went into the house.

"Cli-int!" Mildred's voice was high.

"Yes?"

"Where in the world have you been?"

"Ask the question right. You mean why wasn't I here earlier."

"There's a sandwich and a salad for you in the refrigerator." She came down the stairs.

"Has Miss Franck come in?" he said.

"What ails her?" Mildred said. "She came in about nine—in a big hurry, picked up her things and left. I've had to answer your office bell."

Doc shrugged. His voice was casual. "Well, it doesn't matter." He paused. "Ah—it shouldn't take long to get another one—"

"Just don't expect me to do her work till you get one—that's all."

Doc relaxed. Apparently she didn't know *why* Miss Franck was leaving. "Oh, I wouldn't think of asking you. You're far too busy to help me. It keeps you busy just buying clothes and getting your hair done."

"Well, don't *you* forget we're going to Dr. Eschbach's party tonight."

He stepped down into the office and closed the door. He shuffled through the mail. On one letter was *Church of the Resurrection* and under it *The Rev. Karl Richter, Fair Hill.* Inside would be a personalized check for eight dollars, signed with a flourish. I thought preachers were underpaid; maybe Mary Ann Richter has money—swanky stationery—prompt pay.

The Reverend Karl had been having headaches, was coming along very nicely on Equanil. Doc had to hide the fact that it was a tranquilizer because Richter lashed out in his sermons at the faithless, frantic Americans who gulped so many millions of tranquilizers a year. Not that Doc had heard the sermon; wild horses couldn't drag Doc to Richter's church. Why was it people were supposed to "gulp" tranquilizers? There must be thousands of people who just *took* them.

Doc opened a bottle, shook a large white screw-headed tablet into his hand, and swallowed it. He held a glass under the faucet.

He looked at himself in the mirror. He arched his eyebrows and smiled. He tilted his head, brushed the long black hair back along the temples. Then he took off his dark-rimmed glasses and looked at himself. He put the glasses back on. They *did* add something. He turned back to his desk. That damn Franck girl. Sure it was bad judgment to take her up on the hill, but why let a piece of tail upset your peace of mind. She was gone—for parts unknown, he hoped. What was it Richter had said? "God is the only tranquilizer a man needs." (The Lord is my Miltown, I shall not want—.) "Rev," Doc had said, "your neck muscles are screwed up like a French horn. If there was a God, he wouldn't let a nice guy like you have these headaches. How can you serve Him with your head splitting? You take one of these three times a day and let me know how you feel."

The next day Richter had called. "Slept like a baby, Doctor," he said. "The headaches are gone."

"Well, take it easy a few days, don't work so hard on those sermons."

"Yes, that's what Mrs. Richter says. Doc, is it all right to take these pills every now and then? They certainly work wonders."

"Sure, Rev," said Doc. "Take one with prayers."

So here was the check from the prompt and grateful preacher. Another envelope—a cheap dime-store one—lay on the desk. *Herr* was scribbled in the upper left-hand corner. Doc knew the envelope contained the second half of a payment for a checkup for Anna Herr. Galen Herr never seemed to have quite enough money to pay a bill in full, but he did pay and he always got permission to split the payment. This one would have a cheery note saying something like: "Hi Doc. This cleans it up, hey? *Galen.*"

That optimistic bastard, Doc thought. He's got no money. And he acts like he's got no worries, either. Beaming all the time.

Doc went into the living room, walked to the kitchen, opened the refrigerator, and took out the sandwich and salad Mildred had put there.

"Were there any calls?" he asked.

"That boy that lives in the little stone house next to the church was just here, right before you came—"

"Uh-huh," Doc mumbled, his mouth full. "Kenneth Zercher, what did he want?"

"He said something happened to old Jonas."

The doctor put down his glass of milk. "For God's sake, why didn't you tell me? What did the boy say?"

"He just said you were to come, that something happened to Jonas. He was terribly upset."

Doc Evans grabbed his coat and his black bag, went back into his office, and put some medicine in a vial.

"Do you *have* to go, Clint?" The whine.

"You *know* I do," Clint said.

"Well, try to get back in time to get a little nap so you don't fizzle out at the party by ten."

Doc brought the car to an abrupt halt before the stone cottage. He ran up the path and knocked at the door.

He heard a cry inside. No one came to the door. He rapped sharply on the panel.

He heard the crying again, muffled now. Phares's harsh voice sounded distantly. "You shut up," it said.

"Well, by God," Doc said. "Nobody seems in any hurry."

Phares opened the door.

"The boy said Jonas needed me," Doc said.

"It's been now already almost an hour," Phares said. "If you'd a been where you're supposed to be, maybe you'd be in time oncet."

Doc thrust past Phares. "Where is Jonas?"

"Something came over Jonas in the kitchen. I carried him to the bedroom."

Doc went into the bedroom. Phares followed. "I sent for you right away," Phares said.

Kenneth looked at them from the doorway. Jonas, on the bed, was colorless, thin, without motion. Dr. Evans' face tightened. He opened the slight man's shirt and pressed the stethoscope against the chest.

He listened. "Phares," he said, "he's gone."

Phares stared at the old man. "His old heart give out on him? He was awful short of breath lately."

The doctor fingered Jonas' shirt. Phares stepped forward.

"What's this dark stain, Phares?"

"Stain?" Phares said. "Oh. That. That's soup. Jonas spilled a little tomato soup on himself. He was getting tottery. Kenneth can tell you."

Doc stood. "His heart was certainly under embarrassment—

but I didn't expect this so soon. How old was he exactly—seventy-six?"

"Better," Phares said. "Better than that. He was getting awful old."

Doc bent over the body. "Does he have marks on his neck, Phares? Did he bruise himself?"

Phares stood still. "Marks? Yes, well—ach, I remember. Jonas fell into the washline out back. He said he fell and almost choked himself. He came in and sat on that chair"—Phares drew the doctor from the bedroom into the kitchen— "right there."

"How did he act?" Dr. Evans said.

"Chust like he couldn't get his breath. He breathed big two times and then stopped, didn't seem he ever breathed out. I carried him on the bed and told Kenneth to fetch you."

"All right," Doc said. "You call Charlie Buch—no, I'll do it. I'll probably have to do an autopsy anyhow."

"What for?" Phares said. "What would that be for?"

"Standard procedure," Doc said. "Maybe I won't have to. Where's a phone?"

"In the church," Phares said. "In the office. I'll take you."

"Oh, I can call from home," Doc said.

"Everything all right at home?" Phares said. His heavy, bearded face smiled.

Doc stared at him, picked up his bag, and went out on the porch. Phares followed him and laid a hand on his arm. "It was a heart attack," Phares said. "I saw it myself, Doc."

Doc stepped off the porch. "It was heart, all right. But I thought, if he didn't strain, it would be all right for a while longer."

"It was his heart," Phares said.

"Yes, it was," Doc said. He walked down the path, looking through the rope washlines at the valley spread below. The washlines were at eye level, and Jonas had been just about his height.

5

Hours before Dr. and Mildred Evans rolled out of Fair Hill in their Cadillac, the inhabitants of Fair Hill had the news of Jonas Burkholder's death. Nellie Lehman called Dr. Evans. She'd watched him leave the house. Mary Ann Richter got it from Alma Buch, who called her just after Charlie got the message from the doctor. The news came to Will Shirk's barbershop and spread out from there. Kutz's store had it within an hour and distributed it all afternoon. Finally, everybody knew.

Then another story spread. Chet Lehman had told Nellie that Kenneth had come to him saying, "Come quick, Father is going to hurt Jonas."

"Ach, you must be hearing things," she said, but she repeated it to the neighbors.

Soon phones were ringing. Speculations drifted.

"They say Phares done away with him."

"Well, he always looked to me like he could do such a thing."

By the time Alma Buch had called Mary Ann Richter to ask if she had heard and Mary Ann had told the Reverend Karl, and then had called Nellie Lehman to check up, Charlie Buch was preparing to embalm Jonas' body.

Things were going well. He had shaved Jonas without causing any razor burns, quite a feat for a man who usually cut himself several times each morning. And it was more difficult to shave somebody who couldn't say "ouch." But there had been no annoying interruptions—only one phone call from Phares Zercher, supplying the exact date of Jonas' birth to complete Charlie's information sheet.

Charlie opened a drawer and took out his tools—forceps, scalpel, aneurism hook, bone separator, embalming tubes, and draining tubes. He cut a half-dozen lengths of surgical thread and laid them over the tray. He was going to fill the embalming machine with fluid when he remembered that he had not yet properly closed Jonas' eyes. He selected a pair of eye cups, inserted them, and closed each eye neatly over its cup. Then he took out a pair of rubber gloves, shook them, blew powder into them, and slipped them on his hands. He was leaning over the table to make the incision for the tubes and thinking again, "What a hell of a way to make a living," when there was a knock on the preparation room door.

"Charlie, may I see you?" It was Alma's voice. Charlie put down the scalpel and opened the door. "Here," his wife said, "a cup of coffee for you."

Charlie looked at her. She stood, holding out the cup. It was *her* rule that there should be no spectators and no food and no beverages at an embalming. Alma wouldn't even let Galen Herr witness his work.

"You suddenly snap your cap or something?" asked Charlie, taking the cup.

"Did you notice anything funny about the body? Do you know what people are saying?" said Alma.

Charlie sipped his coffee. "Say that again, Alma: for goodness' sakes, what kind of talk is 'Did I see anything funny, do I know what people are saying'?"

"They say that Jonas didn't just die. They say Phares killed him. Isn't that an awful thing to say?"

"Ay, yi, yi, now who said that?" said Charlie.

"Kenneth's supposed to a ran over to Chet Lehman's and said Phares was killing Jonas."

Charlie took his glasses off and cleaned them with his shirt-tail. He went to the embalming table and looked through the hair for a scalp wound, and over the entire body for bullet or knife holes. He looked closer at marks he had noticed on Jonas' neck while he was shaving him. There were bruises, darker now, on each side of the Adam's apple and a little scratch below the hairline at the back of the neck.

"Do you see anything?" asked Alma from the doorway.

"No," Charlie said, not turning. "No, there's nothing out of the way here. . . . People make up the darnedest things. Anyway, it's not my business to notice these things. Doc Evans said it was heart when he called me."

"Yes," said Alma. "He would know. People sure say some awful things. But Phares is so mean in his heart, you can believe it of him."

"Well," Charlie said, putting the cup down, "I'll tell you something. *I'm* not going to say that Phares did anything like that. He could break me in two with one hand, and he would, too. I saw him pull a fence post out of the ground once. Alma, don't talk any more about it."

"Well, you know I won't. Phares has his weaknesses, I guess. He's mean as sin—" She paused. "And I guess it is true that he sees Suzie Kulp in the church basement, but still I don't believe he'd murder anybody."

"I gotta get back to work," said Charlie. "We have a constable. If they think Phares killed him, why don't they send for Milt Frey?"

"They said they did, but Milt said he wouldn't come on hearsay. Of course, everybody is saying Milt's scared of Phares."

"Who ain't?" said Charlie. "And anyway, the hell with what they say, we want facts."

Alma left the room and Charlie went on with his work.

Galen Herr came out of his house carrying four sleeping bags. In spite of the yelling of his two boys, Butch, five, and Buck, three, he had slept until nine-thirty. He was refreshed. The weather was clear. The weekend was ahead. He tossed the bags into the open rear end of his Ford station wagon. On the lawn, lined up to be packed, were four air mattresses, a three-burner Coleman stove, a length of nylon rope, a lantern, a new 9 by 11 foot umbrella tent bought at a late-season bargain.

Galen stood on the sidewalk and took a deep breath. He looked across the cemetery toward Main Street and across College Avenue to the white schoolhouse. Nice to teach in a white frame schoolhouse; much better than a red brick one—even better when the poplar trees were all there. Why had they cut so many of them down? The way a poplar tree whispers. The falling limbs were a threat to the building and to the kids—can't deny that. Look at the stones in the church, quartz crystals in the stones making them sparkle—was it quartz crystals that did that? Galen looked across the graveyard to the parsonage. Richter, in his study on the second floor, working away at tomorrow's sermon. Galen scanned the tombstones. The big one, *Wagner;* a gray one, *Martin;* all the names were there; no family slighted in that cemetery.

"Hey, Anna," Galen shouted.

Butch, six-gun holsters flapping, came around the corner of the house. "Butch, go tell Mommy to come out."

"O.K., Daddy," said Butch. He ran to the screen door. "Momm-mee, Daddy wants you."

Anna Herr came out of the kitchen with a load of wash carried on the wash-machine lid. She put the lid down and looked up with a frown. She wore one of Galen's shirts and a pair of faded blue Bermudas that barely contained her several months' pregnancy. She was slender, tired looking.

"Come oncet here, Anna," Galen called, waving from the sidewalk.

Anna smiled and put her hands to the small of her back. "O thou false Dutchman," she said, "what nonsense calls me from my domestic appointed rounds?"

"O.K.," Galen said. "That rips it. You stop going Elizabethan, I'll stop going native." He waited for her. "I just wanted you to look at the valley."

"I have been looking at it. It is beautiful, isn't it?"

"It sure is, it almost tempts me to stay home this weekend and take walks from here."

"Oh, there won't be many camping weekends left. You promised the boys."

"I guess you're right," Galen said. "Decisions, decisions. There are just too many wonderful things that need doing."

Anna laughed. "You're always afraid you'll miss something."

"Is that bad?" said Galen.

"Only when you try to milk the maximum—"

"Oh, boy," Galen said. "I'm waiting."

"You want to be sure all the time that you are doing the most wonderful thing possible," Anna said. "Right? You want to play golf but you think, 'This might be the day, if I went fishing I'd catch a coelacanth.' Right? I say that's milking the maximum."

"So, my maximum mammary friend, what?"

"So let's camp on Bear Mountain and not fret because we can't see the dawn come up like thunder out of China 'cross the bay."

"You know, that's what I like about you," said Galen.

She looked at him. "What?"

"You're so homespun," he said.

"Oh, nuts," she said.

"I think this might be the maximum wonderful time to kiss you," he said, taking her in his arms.

"Galen!" She pushed him. "Not out here. Everybody in Fair Hill's got all three eyes—"

Her words were smothered. Buck rang the bell on his fire engine. They jumped. "Now look what you did," said Galen. "You started a fire."

"Boy, we better get a move on," said Anna. "We have more work to do. We'll be lucky to get away before three."

"Aw, you're afraid you'll miss something," Galen said.

Later Galen went up to Kutz's store to buy a mantle for his Coleman lantern. Jake Kutz was unpacking a case of canned soup.

"Well, hello, Mr. Herr," he said, "what can I do for you?"

"Hello, Jake," said Galen. "I need a mantle for my camping lantern. I keep breaking those darn things as fast as I put 'em in."

Jake pulled open a drawer behind the counter and hunted through an assortment of wicks and lantern attachments. "Do you want the large or the medium?" he said.

"Let me look," said Galen. "I've been using the medium, but it's only a single-mantle lantern, maybe I better try a large one —oh, I'll take both. The way I ruin these things, I'll need 'em."

"Anything else?" Jake asked.

"No, that will be all," said Galen.

Jake ran up the sale and handed change to Galen.

"That's too bad about Jonas Burkholder," he said.

Galen frowned. "What happened to Jonas?"

"Oh, then you didn't know. Why, he died, oh, I guess about two, three hours ago."

Galen stared. "Why, I saw him just this morning taking a walk with the Zercher boy, and I said to Anna that Jonas was looking pretty strong."

"Yes, well," said Jake, "heart's a funny thing. You can look good and"—he snapped his fingers—"you're gone just like that."

"Oh, then it was his heart?" said Galen.

"Yes," said Jake. "They had Doc Evans. He said it was heart. Well, one thing's for sure, we'll miss him."

"Yes," said Galen. "Everybody liked him. It'll be a big funeral. About when do you think they'll bury him?"

"Oh, I judge Monday or Tuesday," Jake said. "They don't keep 'em as long as they used to."

"No," Galen said, "no, they don't."

Galen walked down the street. Jonas Burkholder was dead. Well, he was an old man. But Kenneth—Jonas meant a lot to Kenneth.

As Galen approached the sexton's house, he tried to decide whether or not he should stop in. It was hard to tell how Phares would take such a visit. The right thing to do was to stop. If he wasn't welcome he'd leave. At least he'd have done his part.

He went around the side of the house and knocked softly on the kitchen door. At once he heard a frightened sobbing, and then a low gruff voice.

"All right, stop it. Everytime someone raps on the door you start blubbering. Now quit or I'll—"

Galen rapped again a little harder.

Phares opened the door and stood big in the doorway.

"I heard about Jonas," Galen said. "I stopped to say I am sorry and see if there's anything I can do to help."

Phares stared. "Ha, I never saw so goddam many people trying to feel sorry and makin' out like they want to help something. Now what the hell would there be to help?"

"Well," Galen said, "you'll have to dig a grave. We could take care of Kenneth."

"Ha," said Phares. "It won't take me no time to throw out a grave, and the boy can take care of himself. Now you chust go on home, and if you run into any people coming this way, you tell them to do their good by minding their own business for a change."

As Phares slammed the door, Galen saw Kenneth, pale and frightened, standing in the far corner of the kitchen.

Galen walked home through the cemetery.

Anna was in the kitchen separating the wash into piles. One pile that needed to be ironed, second pile that didn't need to be ironed. Most women in Fair Hill ironed everything—socks, dish cloths, cleaning rags. The rule was simple. If you washed it, you ironed it. If there was a lot of it, you got up early and stayed up till it was done. Anna broke the rule. She ironed pants and shirts. Only. And maybe.

"Anna," Galen said, "I guess we better not try a camping trip this weekend."

"Well, you promised," Anna said. "I don't care; I have a lot to do. But the boys'll be disappointed."

"Jonas Burkholder died," Galen said. "I think I ought to stay around."

"Jonas died! It's a wonder you didn't wait awhile to tell me," Anna said. The telephone rang in the living room. Anna answered it. Galen went to the kitchen window and gazed across the cemetery and the western portion of the valley. Phares Zercher came into the cemetery carrying a pick and a shovel. He walked to the southwestern corner. He walked fast. He stopped beneath the big white oak, the largest tree on the plot Jonas had bought many years ago. Phares marked off his work, stripped away the turf, and began to loosen the ground with his pick.

Anna entered the kitchen, her eyes bright.

Galen looked at her. "Now, don't tell me; let me guess—they caught Karl Richter shacking up with Suzie Kulp in the church belfry?"

"Oh, Galen," Anna said. "That was Mary Ann Richter on the phone."

"Um," said Galen, "then, let me see. Nellie Lehman does regular Thursday night volunteer work for the Red Rose chapter of Destitute Prostitutes of America."

"Be serious a minute, Galen," said Anna. "This is terrible and it's not just gossip. It's too serious for that."

"I'm sorry, Anna," he said. "Tell me."

"It's about Jonas. They say he didn't just die. They say Phares killed him."

"Good Lord, Anna. How could anyone know that?"

"Kenneth Zercher ran over to Chet Lehman's. He was white as a sheet and he said, 'Come quick, I think Pop's going to kill Uncle Jonas.' Well, Chet went over. I guess he didn't go right away and he rapped on the door and nobody answered for a while and then Phares is supposed to have opened the door and said Jonas had a little spell and he was going to send for Doc Evans."

"The doctor came, didn't he?"

"Yes, I guess he did and Jonas was dead."

"Jake Kutz told me Doc Evans said he died of a heart attack."

"Yes, but some people say Doc wasn't there long enough to make a close check, and why would Kenneth run over to Chet like that? You don't just run out and say, 'Pop's gonna kill Jonas' for the heck of it, do you? They say Phares always did want Jonas' house. I heard that many a time."

"Well, Anna, I don't know. The boy's sensitive. I have him in school. He has a good imagination. He might have misunderstood or something. I'd want to be sure before I'd say that anybody killed anybody—especially Phares Zercher."

"They say Chet Lehman's half scared to death. Nellie told it to the neighbors, you know, without thinking, and Chet's afraid Phares'll kill *him* if it gets back that Chet spread something like that. So Chet's starting to say it didn't happen that way. And everybody's supposed not to say they heard it from Chet."

"It sure is a hell of a thing," Galen said. He looked out the window across the cemetery to where Phares was digging Jonas' grave. Phares was already dug in past his knees. Down went the shovel, up went the dirt, the pile of brown earth growing. Down, up; down, up. "Well, why don't they do an autopsy then and find out what killed him?"

"I don't know anything about these things," Anna said. "I'm just telling you what they say."

6

By agreement of all people immediately concerned—Phares Zercher, Charlie Buch, Karl Richter—it was possible to schedule Jonas' funeral for 2 P.M. on Monday. Phares as "surviving family" and gravedigger urged an early funeral. Charlie Buch had no other bodies to prepare, Reverend Richter was available, as was the church; there were no distant relatives to notify; so, though it seemed hasty to many, there was no compelling reason to wait.

It was to be a public church funeral; news of the details spread throughout Fair Hill and the valley.

The day was fair, with sudden gusts that shook windows and made people hold their hats.

Not everybody came to the funeral. Doc Evans wasn't there; he had to spend the afternoon at the county hospital. A few Hillians sat at the hotel bar as usual.

But most people were there. All the seats were filled in the old stone building. People stood in the aisle and in the rear. The loft overhead was opened and even that was filled to capacity.

In front of the altar, the coffin rested on a wheeled carrier, surrounded by banks of flowers. Fragrance drifted through the church.

Sounds of restrained breathing, an occasional cough, a rustle of clothing were all that broke the silence. An usher tiptoed up the west aisle and opened two windows to let in the papery whisper of the poplar leaves that flickered in the sunlight like a thousand hazy mirrors. A pallbearer whispered to Charlie Buch, who nodded vigorously, breaking for a brief moment the solemn mask he wore. Phares Zercher sat stiff in the front pew in his shapeless black suit, which tightened as he breathed. He gazed ahead, oblivious to glances and whispers and stares. Beside him Kenneth sat, studying the floor. Farther back near a window sat Suzie Kulp, relaxed, chewing gum. Though she hadn't talked to Phares since Friday night, she wasn't asking the question the others were asking. She knew. He would get away with it. The story about Kenneth and Chet Lehman was just some more Fair Hill gossip. Phares would not have been stupid enough to do it in front of the boy. It would blow over —hadn't they once said that she had got rid of a baby?

Near the back of the church sat Galen Herr, trying to understand the meaning Jonas' death had. He and Anna had talked about it; he had thought long about it walking up to Zimmerman's Hill the day before to look at the valley. Why did the whole town come to the funeral of an old man who had only one blood relative left in the world? There was no great grief, no loud sobbing. . . . These people knew about death. There was even something beautiful about it, especially the death of an old man, especially a good old man—a sense of refreshment, a well-earned rest. Why then the heavy sense of loss? Had all these people thought about it? Some words of a poem formed into his mind.

> Into the darkness they go, the wise and lovely—
> Gently they go, the beautiful, the tender, the kind.

Other lines, another poem:

And a thousand slimy things lived on and so did I.

"Maybe this is it," he thought. "The good things are going and the slimy things are staying." When Galen first came to Fair Hill, Doc Wagner was the doctor. Bowman was the preacher. Harry Reist was the undertaker. Galen's own predecessor, John Brindle, had taught English and Latin in the Fair Hill School for thirty-four years. The things Brindle's pupils had learned still echoed in their minds. On a subzero morning one might hear Hank Wetzel, the milkman, slap his mittens together and say to an early riser, " 'A cold no coat however stout of homespun stuff could quite shut out'—John Brindle made me learn that damn thing when I was in school. I always think of it cold mornings like this."

Wagner, Bowman, Reist, Brindle—all gone now.

Jonas Burkholder seemed the symbol of all that was good in the old. Jonas taught without entering the school. Without taking the pulpit, he preached. Without drugs, he healed, and he lovingly prepared the final resting places of his friends.

So long as Jonas lived there was no sense of loss. But now Jonas was dead—and a thousand slimy things lived on.

When the good land washes little by little into the crooked creek and the yellowed stones appear, how are the seeds nourished? Maybe Richter will say something about savor restored to salt. He hoped. Our Savior and our savor.

Galen smiled. He could almost hear Jonas. "Ach, Galen," he would say, "don't you know there's never any more or less of good or bad. It just gets piled up sometimes in some places and it gets scarce in others for a while and then things even out."

Maybe that was the way it was, and then again, maybe that wasn't the way it was.

This ugly rumor about Phares. Was there anything to do about that?

Promptly at two, Karl Richter, black-robed, came to the pulpit.

"I am the resurrection and the life, saith the Lord. *He that believeth in me, though he were dead, yet shall he live—"*

Taking liberty with the order of the services, he began a funeral eulogy of Jonas.

"For man walketh in a vain shadow and disquieteth himself in vain. He heapeth up riches and cannot tell who shall gather them." Richter was careful not to look at Phares. He went to the next reading.

"I will lift up mine eyes unto the hills, from whence cometh my help.

". . . Our brother, Jonas, lived on the hill as most of us do. Everywhere he looked on the hill he saw the handiwork of God. You dwellers in the valley would do well to pause from time to time and look at the hill and find your help there. Let me say also that our brother Jonas got his help from the valley. Every day of his life he could be seen walking the ridge below the cemetery or sitting on the bench behind his house looking at the beautiful valley of the crooked creek—and finding God there. It wasn't very long ago Jonas said to me right under the big elm back of the church, 'If when the going gets tough people would just stop long enough to take a long look at the valley, they would find God there and they wouldn't have to go to the hotel for beer.' "

Galen Herr squirmed in his seat. Jonas never said a thing like that. Was it right to put words in a dead man's mouth? Or was it possible that Richter was giving an honest account of what he thought he had heard Jonas say? Was Jonas in his tolerance and wisdom all things to all people? Dead only two days, Jonas was already a myth.

"Yes, my friends, Jonas loved the valley. He loved it so well he even wrote poetry about it. Yesterday I was going through the table drawer in the sexton's room in the basement and I found this." He held up a piece of paper. "Written in Jonas' handwriting—I'd like to read it to you as a tribute to the talent and sensitivity of our departed brother." He cleared his throat. "It's called 'My Valley!'

> My Valley, white in winter, green in spring,
> And gold on summer's long, limp days—
> I taste the sweet breath you sigh at dawn
> And listen to the sadness of your soul
> At evening when the sun goes down.
> Dear Valley, you are soft and sweet and cool,
> But I am in no rush to sleep within your bosom.
> I'm yet content to walk and look and love.

Richter repeated softly, " 'I am in no rush to sleep within your bosom.' " A woman sobbed.

"Yes, my beloved, can we appreciate this gentle old man turning his spirit to poetry in the quietness of the very heart of this church? This man knew the beauty of the mortality we all share."

Parishioners glanced toward Phares, who sat completely still. Some eyes turned to Suzie Kulp, who sat without expression, sunlight and leaf shadows playing on her throat.

"Oh, my friends—how great a loss is this! We have lost here more than a sexton. We have lost a philosopher, a friend, yes, even a saint."

The Reverend Richter paused, took off his glasses, polished them with a handkerchief drawn from beneath his robe, wiped his face and the corner of an eye. He closed the book slowly.

"If there are any who have not viewed the remains, they may do so now. The service will be concluded at the grave."

Galen Herr was glad the sermon was over—to read a dead man's personal poem—to misquote him—as if showing the dead clay were not enough to do to a man. But the people of Fair Hill didn't feel this way. They didn't know what to make of the poem. They rather liked that Richter had read it. As for viewing, that wasn't indignity, that was honor. They filed past the bier, pausing to admire the flowers and Charlie Buch's art, though there were some lamented that Buch never could get the restful look that Harry Reist used to achieve.

"My, doesn't he look thin?" a viewer said.

"Yes, but so natural," another said.

"Well, he went sudden. I always think that helps."

In groups of two, three, and four, the people slowly left the church and walked toward the grave. The pallbearers closed the lid and carried the coffin to the hearse to be transported down the driveway to the graveside.

Phares Zercher came out of the church, told Kenneth to go ahead, and then walked across the lawn to where Suzie Kulp stood. He stopped beside her and looked at her.

"Why, Phares," she said, "you look awful. Your hair's not combed and your beard's rough. I never seen you look so bad."

Phares ran his tongue across his upper lip. "I didn't sleep so good these last two nights. That's the first time in my life I didn't sleep right away—"

"Phares," Suzie murmured, "I'm proud of you. I didn't think that the next time I seen you it'd be Jonas' funeral."

"I will be glad when it's over," said Phares. "I dug the grave deep. You know, Suzie, I hear him breathe sometimes."

"He'll be in the ground tonight, Phares. You won't hear him. Maybe you can see me in the basement tonight and we can talk about what we'll do."

"Once I even got up in the night and went to his room to see if he was there. For a minute I thought it hadn't happened. But he wasn't there."

"Well, you'll soon forget that," said Suzie. "I'll see to that. You have nothing to worry about."

"Do the people talk, Suzie?" Phares stopped. "It seems the people look at me funny. It wonders me what they think."

"People talk in Fair Hill," said Suzie. "They find something to say." She paused. "Phares, Kenneth wasn't there, was he?"

Phares drew breath. "Yes, he was there, why?"

"The people say he ran over to Chet Lehman and told Chet you were killing Jonas. You weren't dumb enough to do this in front of the boy, Phares?"

"I got mad. I didn't want to do it just then. I was going to wait till he took his nap, but he made me mad and that scared Kenneth and he ran out the door."

"Good God, Phares, you are in for it. What will you do?"

"The boy says he only told Chet to come, there was something wrong with Jonas. But he must of said more." Phares waited. "Chet should not say anything if he knows what's good."

"Yes, that's it, Phares. I know Chet is scared already. If you can keep him that way and keep Kenneth quiet, it will all blow over."

"Well, I can do that. Ach, there are so many things I didn't think about." He rubbed his beard. "I wish I had it to do over."

"Don't talk like that, Phares," Suzie said. "It's done."

By this time the people were nearly all assembled in a group by the graveside. The pallbearers had placed the casket on the straps of the chrome frame that was to lower Jonas' body to the bottom.

"You better go now," said Suzie. "I'll tell you if I hear something else."

The wind from the valley grew stronger. It turned coat lapels up and hat brims down. It whipped through the flowers and got beneath the green rug of artificial grass that covered the pile of brown earth. The onionskin pages of Reverend Richter's little black book snicked as he read, "*Man that is born of woman hath but a short time to live and is full of misery. He cometh up and is cut down like a flower. He fleeth as it were a shadow.*"

Someone crossed two small flowers on the coffin, and Richter sprinkled a handful of earth over it. "Earth to earth, ashes to ashes, dust to dust."

Charles Buch pushed a button. A little motor hummed and the chrome bars began to turn. The coffin descended slowly; the people watched.

Into Galen Herr's mind, verse came again, uninvited. A poem in the junior English textbook. He had read it so often it came whole to his mind.

I am not resigned to the shutting away of loving hearts in the hard ground.
So it is, and so it will be, for so it has been time out of mind:
Into the darkness they go, the wise and the lovely. Crowned
With lilies and with laurel they go; but I am not resigned.

Lovers and thinkers, into the earth with you,
Be one with the dull, the indiscriminate dust.
A fragment of what you felt, of what you knew,
A formula, a phrase remains—but the best is lost.

The answers quick and keen, the honest look, the laughter, the love,—
They are gone. They are gone to feed the roses. Elegant and curled
Is the blossom. Fragrant is the blossom. I know. But I do not approve.
More precious was the light in your eyes than all the roses of the world.

Down, down, down into the darkness of the grave
Gently they go, the beautiful, the tender, the kind;
Quietly they go, the intelligent, the witty, the brave.
I know. But I do not approve. And I am not resigned.

The coffin came to the bottom of the grave. The motor stopped humming and Richter said, "Let us pray."

It was over. The people left in groups, talking about the weather and work still to do that day to make up for the time off.

Charles Buch began to collect his equipment.

Phares Zercher went into the house to change clothes before coming back and filling in the grave. Chet Lehman stood looking at the valley, at the ball diamond, and at the sky. Galen Herr walked around the cemetery looking at the stones of Doc Wagner, Reverend Bowman, Harry Reist, John Brindle, fighting the sorrow he felt at the graveside. Jonas was old. He'd had a good life. He had a heart attack and he died without pain. What more do you want? Even if it hadn't been a heart attack. Suppose Phares had killed him. So Doc Evans wasn't the doctor that Wagner was, nor Galen Herr the teacher John Brindle was. So what was he to do about it? He saw Chet Lehman walking.

"Chet," said Galen, "Chet, I have a question maybe you can answer."

Chet looked at him. Finally, he said, "Well, if I can I guess I'd be glad to answer something. To tell you the truth I waited off to the side here so I wouldn't need to talk. I just don't feel like talking. You know. Jonas was a good neighbor."

"Yes," Galen said, pulling a blade of sweet grass and chewing it. "Well, there's just something I have to know, I guess. You know what the people are saying, don't you?"

"Well, I guess not—no. No, I can't say I know what the people say," Chet said.

"They say that Jonas didn't have a heart attack. They say Phares killed him." Galen watched Chet. "I just wondered if you have any reason to believe what they say."

Phares Zercher came out of the sexton's house, picked up the shovel from the porch, and started toward the grave. When he saw Galen and Chet, he stopped and glared at them.

"I wouldn't say a thing like that," Chet said. "It wouldn't be healthy for me to say such a thing. And it might not be so good for you to ask the question."

"But you're not saying it isn't so, are you?"

Lehman stared at the ground.

"What did Kenneth Zercher say to you on Saturday?" Galen said.

"Who said Kenneth came running over? And if he did, I

don't think I could say exactly what he said. I have to go. Nellie will want me to do some things."

Chet walked away. Galen stared after him. Then Galen turned toward the house. Out of the corner of his eye he could see Phares stop his shoveling and look after him.

7

"Will Kenneth be home for dinner?" Suzie closed the door behind her. Phares looked up. He pushed the German Bible away from him across the kitchen table.

"I wish still you'd rap when you come," he said.

"Oh, I'm sorry I scared you," she said. "I just thought if Kenneth carried his lunch again today, I'd stop in and make our dinner. There are some things we must talk over."

Phares looked at the kitchen clock—eleven-thirty. "He carried his lunch all right. He hardly eats anything in this house any more."

"Well, no wonder; you have him half scared to death." Suzie walked to the refrigerator. "I'll warm up the *rivel* soup I made the other day, and I'll fry you some scrapple. What do you think?"

Phares grunted and leaned back; the chair creaked. "I have to keep him scared. He has to keep his mouth shut; he could spoil everything. The Goat Woman said that chust the other day. She said, 'Watch the boy'; that's all she tells me any more."

"Oh, Phares," Suzie said. She shook her head as she cut several thick slices from the block of scrapple. "Now, you didn't go to her again. What could the Goat Woman tell you now? What do you want her to tell you?"

Phares leaned forward heavily; the chair legs dug into the linoleum. He slapped the table. "She could say that things are going to be all right. She knows these things."

"Ach, what does she know?" Suzie said, laying the slices in the popping grease.

"Well, I got the house, didn't I? She knew that, didn't she?"

"Sure, she knew it," Suzie said. "She knew it because Ezra Weinhold told her. Right after Jonas had his spell he went to Ezra and had the house willed to you, and Ezra told the Goat Woman. That's how she knew."

Phares shook his head. "I don't believe it. She did it with seeds. She had a whole lot of different kinds in saucers."

Suzie turned the flame down under the pan. "Oh, Phares," she said, "*Ich mane es kann net sei.* It can't be that you believe such things."

"Yes, well, people think what they have to think, but I *know.*"

Suzie set the table then and they began to eat.

"It chust stands to reason," Phares said. "If the boy says he saw something that day, there could be trouble. And if *he* says nothing, then who else knows anything? Even if Chet Lehman does say some things—well, if Kenneth says that's not the way it was, then what is there to worry about? No, I think the Goat Woman has right, there. I must watch Kenneth. Why, chust last night again he was talking in his sleep, and I went over and slapped him awake."

"What did he say, Phares?" Suzie asked.

"Well, it was bad enough; let me tell you that."

"Now, Phares, you look at me," Suzie pointed a finger at him. "I work in a lot of homes. I hear what people say." Phares listened, rubbing his beard. "And one thing they notice is that you act like a guilty man. You lay awake all night and try to hear Jonas breathe or try to hear if Kenneth mumbles something in his sleep, and then when you do hear these things you walk around the next day watching people to see if they heard it too."

"Ach, you talk like a man up a tree."

"No, I make sense," Suzie said, "and you better listen. Joe Bixler said it just the other day; he said you come in the post office and look at people like you want to read their mind. It's just gettin' so people don't want to meet you on the street."

"Well, and how do they look at me?" Phares said, putting his big hands flat on the table and looking up at Suzie through his bushy brows. "They look at me and I can tell what they think. They think to themselves, 'There's the man that done away with that nice old man.' Why, chust the other day, there was some boys on the ball diamond. I was taking some leaves down to the cut, and they yelled, 'Hey, killer!' at me—"

"So I heard. That's just what I mean. And what did you do? You chased them across the ball diamond and threw stones at them. That's no way, Phares; now all the boys will start teasing you, and this thing will just never blow over."

A vein stood out on Phares's forehead. "Well, if I ever catch one; if I ever catch one."

Suzie spoke quickly. "That's no way; now you listen to me." She came to Phares, put her hands around his head, and pulled him toward her. "Look, you have the house; you have the job; when things settle down a little we'll get married and live here. There are just two things you got to do. Are you listening, Phares?" Phares nodded. "You must not keep Kenneth so scared. If he goes to school every day white as a sheet and can't recite his lessons, they'll start asking him questions. It's better if you can get him to think that nothing happened after he ran out of the house that day—that you didn't keep on holding onto Jonas, you know. The quicker he gets to seem normal again the better." Phares nodded. "And the other thing is Chet

Lehman," Suzie said. "You must do just the opposite with him. Right now people don't know what to think. There's some think that maybe Kenneth *did* run over and tell Chet, 'Come quick, Pop's killing Jonas.' But some think that's just some more Fair Hill gossip. And most people don't know what to think." Suzie dropped her hands and stepped back. "The thing is this: if Chet thinks things are cooling off, he might be tempted to tell somebody something that would stir things all up again. So, what you have to do is keep Chet scared—but just Chet, Phares, not the whole town. Do you understand?"

Phares stood up, nodding. "You have a good understanding. I will try." He clenched and unclenched his fists. "I've been watching Chet Lehman—that little *Menischte*—I can take care of him."

Suzie looked at Phares sharply. "But you mustn't lose your temper." She sighed and looked at the clock. "Well, I must go soon." She poured hot water from the teakettle into the dishpan, washed the dishes in silence, and left.

That evening at supper Phares tried to carry out Suzie's advice concerning Kenneth. He tried not to look at the boy too harshly, and he didn't speak through the uneasy meal. When they had finished, Phares said, "It's all right if you go to your room right away. I'll redd up the kitchen." Kenneth looked surprised but accepted the chance eagerly.

When the dishes were done, Phares sat by the window in the parlor and watched the walk leading from Chet Lehman's back porch to his garage. Sooner or later Chet would go to his workshop in the garage to repair a lock, file a saw, or do some other task.

A triangle of light from the Lehman kitchen flooded the lawn. Chet came down the rear steps of the house. Phares moved to the front porch of the sexton's house. By the time he got there, Chet was closing the door behind him in the garage.

Phares strode across the street. He ducked beneath the

kitchen window so that Nellie wouldn't see him and hurried to the garage door. He stood, listening to a filing sound inside. Then he wrenched the door open so violently the suction rattled the window above Chet's head. Phares stooped to clear the lintel of the small opening. Chet looked up from the piece of pipe held in the vise. When he saw Phares, the color left his cheeks. Phares moved to him quickly and grabbed the lapels of Chet's woolen button-up sweater.

"What's this you are telling people about me?" Phares said intensely, his bearded face within inches of Chet's faded lips.

"Wha—what talk? I—I didn't," Lehman gasped.

"You know damned well what I mean." Phares lifted Chet off his feet. Behind Chet a twenty-penny nail stuck out from a stud about six feet above the floor. Phares hung him on it by the sweater and shirt now pulled up under Chet's arms. Chet cried out as the head of the nail bit into his back. Phares stood back and watched him dangle, arms flailing as the nail bent slowly and the garments began to tear. Buttons popped and Chet fell, sitting, to the floor, leaving the sweater hanging on the nail. Phares kicked him. Chet fell over.

"Now, you better watch what you say the next time somebody asks you what Kenneth said to you the day Jonas died. Do you understand?"

"Yes, yes," Chet said, panting. "I never said anything bad about you, Phares. And I never will."

Phares placed a heavy boot an inch from Chet's face. "If you do, I'll pull your arms off one by one. *Versteh?* Maybe I'll do it anyway, *versteh?*"

"I understand, Phares. You can trust me," Chet whispered.

"And if you tell anybody I was over here tonight, you'll get the same thing again." Phares turned and left.

Chet Lehman picked himself up and went into the house. When Nellie saw him, she dropped her dish towel and ran to him with a chair. "For goodness' sakes, Chester. What's wrong with you?"

"I fe–fell–d-down the ladder from–second-floor garage."

"Oh, now you didn't, ach, my, Chester; shall I call Doc?"

"No," Chet gasped, "just help me to bed; I don't feel so good."

8

Galen Herr tossed his brief case into the corner and slumped into the chair. Anna watched him.

"Teaching didn't used to tire you like this. Lately you come home bushed. What's wrong?" Galen, silent, looked across the cemetery. "Maybe you ought to have Doc Evans look you over."

Galen smiled faintly. "Don't look so worried, Anna. There's nothing wrong with me that a doctor could help."

"A little sherry?"

"No, it's not that kind of problem either. . . . It's just that teaching doesn't go right lately. I seem to have lost—well—my purpose. It sounds a lot worse than it is, really. It'll come back."

Anna said, "I'm not sure I understand."

Galen leaned forward. "Take today in English class—the junior class—somebody mentioned *For Whom the Bell Tolls* and I started to explain how Hemingway got the title from John Donne—you know, 'any man's death diminishes me, because I am involved in mankind; and therefore never send to know for whom the bell tolls; it tolls for thee.' I like to talk about that poem—usually—but today all I could think of was Jonas Burkholder dead and those damn rumors, and my mind was a complete blank; I just couldn't say anything; I haven't felt like that since the first day I did practice-teaching."

"What did you do?"

"I gave them the rest of the time for study. Good thing it was the last period."

"Well, it doesn't sound too serious," Anna said.

"It's serious if Phares killed Jonas. Shouldn't somebody do something about it?"

"Galen, hardly anybody thinks seriously about these rumors. They say that Kenneth didn't even go over to Chet Lehman's house that day. It'd be one thing if there were some substantial evidence, but—" Anna shook her head.

"I know what the people say," Galen said. "They're mighty eager to believe whatever makes it easy for them, but Chet Lehman slinks around like a scared cat; some folks notice that too. Have you ever put the question right to him?" Anna shook her head. "Well, try it, see what you think. And there's Kenneth. Today when I called the class off after I choked up, I looked at him and the tears were streaming down his cheeks. Why would that be? He's pale and he can't concentrate. I don't dare call on him in class. And just now when school let out I stopped him a minute, and I said, 'Is something wrong?' and he turned white and stammered that I mustn't ask him that and then he ran across the cemetery."

"It's a dreadful thing," Anna said. "I don't know what you can do. I'll tell you one thing: I don't think you ought to badger that child. You might do more harm than good." She turned to go toward the kitchen. "I must get supper on."

Galen followed her. "You're right, Anna. But don't I have a responsibility to Kenneth? He's my student. And he's suffering. And he doesn't have Jonas any more. What am I supposed to do? Ignore him?"

"No," Anna said, "you have a responsibility—a responsibility to be concerned, to be upset, to be worried. But you don't have a responsibility to play coroner, constable, or God." She waved the paring knife. "And you don't have any responsibility to get Phares Zercher on your neck and make me a widow. Now go take a long walk and get it out of your system."

Galen shrugged and climbed the stairs. A few minutes later he came down in old trousers and a heavy sweatshirt. "What you said makes sense," he said. "I'll take that walk and think about it." He kissed her on the cheek and left.

Outside autumn was in the air. Bright leaves were swirling; corn stalks in Levi Martin's field were turning brown. Galen walked out along the ridge past Jonas' grave; stopped by the big oak and looked at the valley; and then, skirting left field of the ball diamond, followed the cut down to Noah Weber's farm. Fence row led to fence row—south to the Crooked Creek, east to the Earltown Road, north to the concrete block works, and Levi Martin's lane home.

Galen and Anna lingered over coffee while the boys played cowboy around the yard. When Anna started to wash the dishes, Galen took a dish cloth and offered to dry them.

"So the walk didn't solve the problem," Anna said.

"Not completely," Galen said.

"What will you do next?"

"As soon as we finish the dishes and get the kids to bed, I think I'll go up to Reverend Richter's."

"What do you think you can learn from him?"

Galen rubbed a hand over his crew-cut hair. "He lives next door to Phares, sees Phares every day, people tell him things—and he's sly. Maybe he knows something."

Anna blew a lock of hair out of her eye. "If you have no more respect for him than that—"

"Oh, he's all right," Galen said. "It's just that I've listened to him. Somebody asks him a fair question and he looks up and says, 'There is no ceiling to God's love' or 'The Lord will provide' or 'Let us not forget, Christ is the ruler yet.' And then the person looks into that earnest face and thinks Richter has said something profound."

"And," Anna said, "the person goes home and ponders the remark and, lo, it *was* profound."

"That's right," Galen said, laughing, "and the only question remaining is 'Did Richter know it?'" He went to the closet, took out a cap and jacket. "Anyway, I hope he gives me something to ponder."

"Send the boys in when you go out," Anna said. "I'll put them to bed."

Galen went into the yard and looked around for the boys. Just as he opened his mouth to call them, they burst around the corner in full cowboy regalia. Buck's two pistols strapped to his legs were almost as big as he was. When the two children saw Galen, they skidded to a halt in front of him and both went for their guns.

"All right, hands up, you dirty rustler," cried Butch. But Buck was taking no chances. He fanned the hammer wildly, pumping bullets into the bad man although the heavy barrel was pointing almost at his feet.

"I gotcha; I gotcha," he yelled.

"Good work, boys," Galen said, shaking hands with them. "You got the rustlers before bedtime. It's pretty hard to spot 'em after dark."

The boys holstered their guns.

"Now into the bunkhouse, men," Galen said. "You guys sure earned your rest today; a man works hard all day catching rustlers deserves his sleep."

The boys dashed in the front door.

Galen could hear Butch yell, "Mom, open the bunkhouse; we earned our rest." The boys might go to bed promptly without a fight.

Instead of taking the short cut through the cemetery Galen

took the longer route up College Avenue to Main Street. The air was still; Fair Hill was quiet.

Mary Ann Richter answered Galen's ring at the parsonage. She smiled at him, her brown eyes glistening behind polished rimless glasses.

"Oh, come in, Mr. Herr," she said. "I suppose you've come to see Reverend Richter?" Galen nodded. "He's up in his study. He'll be glad to see you."

Mary Ann was large-boned and full-fleshed. She was the kind that aged early, whereas her husband was perennially youthful and would have looked four years younger than she even if they had been the same age. To narrow the gap Mary Ann used a little more lipstick than Fair Hill thought proper for a preacher's wife.

"It's getting a little like fall out, isn't it?" she said, as she hung up Galen's cap and jacket.

A carpeted open stairway led to the second floor; the darkened living room was on the right and the kitchen at the end of the hall to the rear. At the sound of voices, the Reverend Richter appeared at the top of the stairs. He wore his usual dark blue suit and dark tie.

"Hello, Galen, come on up."

Inside the study Richter offered Galen the easy chair, then turned his desk chair around.

"It's nice to have a chance to talk with you," Richter said. His voice was precise. Galen looked at the bookcases, the couch, the farmhouse lights blinking in the valley.

"I wanted to talk with you," Galen said. "To get your opinion on something that's been bothering me."

Richter crossed his legs. "That's what I'm here for—to talk with people who are bothered."

Galen leaned forward. "It's about Jonas Burkholder's death —the stories that are going around."

Richter pushed his lower lip forward, looked at the ceiling, and drew in a breath. "What I mean is," Galen said, "I think somebody in Fair Hill ought to find out for sure."

Richter frowned. He leaned back, his hands on the chair arms.

"I've done a lot of thinking about this. A number of people think somebody ought to do something."

"And what do *you* think?" Galen asked.

Richter blinked, his flat face blank. "Well, first, there's always a great deal of idle talk in towns the size of Fair Hill. They're all alike. I was born in one, went to school in another, and the few years I've been here show that this one is just like the rest." He brought his hands to his lap and leaned forward. "My goodness, Galen, these people have imaginations. Most of the people in this town still believe in ghosts. Now I'm of German descent too, and where I come from we tell ghost stories, but here they *believe* them. Doc Evans told me himself that some of the people have more faith in powwow doctors than they do in him. They're just too ready to believe things, and you know as well as I do how they can supply missing details."

Galen shook his head. "I'm beginning to think in this case it's the other way around. People pass this story around; but they don't *believe* it—at least not enough to stand by it. Weren't the people who talked to you about this eager to give up after you told them it was idle gossip?"

"Without exception," Richter said, nodding. "They all seemed relieved. I grant you that."

"That's right," Galen said, "when it comes to deciding whether one should be generous and forgiving—you know, hear no evil, see no evil—or hunt the truth and maybe get somebody as mean and tough as Phares Zercher on his neck, everyone decides that the Christian thing to do is believe the best. And that's what has me worried. Man, I want to believe that you can't believe anything you hear."

Richter shifted. "Well, if you're asking me, Did Phares kill

Jonas? I don't know. I really don't know. So I just assume that the people who have responsibility in these matters get the facts and act accordingly."

"You mean Milt Frey?"

Richter nodded. "And Doc Evans; he's the coroner."

"Do you know what Milt Frey says? He says, 'Let somebody charge Phares, I'll pick him up. I can't go around arresting people on suspicions.' "

"He's within his rights there," Richter said. "There just aren't enough facts. Who'd dare to have Phares arrested and then have the case thrown out for lack of evidence? Then there *would* be a murder."

"Well, Reverend, why do *you* think Kenneth ran over to Chet Lehman? What do *you* think he said to Chet?"

Richter shrugged. "Chet says that's not so."

"He didn't deny it when I asked him after the funeral. And have you seen him lately? He walks around like a man afraid of his shadow."

The preacher nodded. "How about Kenneth?"

Galen shook his head. "I tried him. Nothing. Does a Pennsylvania Dutch boy go against his father? Does a Kenneth go against a Phares? But why does Kenneth go around numb and white all the time? What is tormenting him so?"

Richter gazed at Galen. He leaned back. "Well, *vengeance is mine, saith the Lord;* I guess you'll just have to let Him handle it."

"And while He's working on it, maybe there are a few things we could be doing."

"What?" Richter said. "Exactly?"

"Phares himself," Galen said. "Maybe if enough of us confront him, we could get the truth from him. There'd be some safety in numbers."

A shadow passed behind the Reverend Richter's eyes. "What a preposterous idea! For heaven's sake, Galen, confront him with what?"

Galen ran his fingers through his stubby hair. "Oh, I don't know. Evidence. Trumped-up evidence. Marks on the body. Phares isn't smart. He's a nervous, superstitious brute. Scare him, he'd give himself away. I often see a light in his kitchen half the night. They say he goes to see the Goat Woman."

"That's true enough. She has the *Hexerei* on him; if there's anything like it." Richter turned his face toward the ceiling. "He told me right after he got the house; he said, 'The old devil knows the truth.' I told him he'd do better to get his truth in church."

"What did he say to that?"

The preacher sniffed, lowered his head, and smiled. "He just said, 'Ach, Reverend, there just ain't enough truth there for people like me. I tried,' he said, 'to get some out of Jonas' Bible, but there just ain't enough to go around; it's just a lot of words and no sense.' Now, what do you do with such ignorance?" Richter shook his head.

"It shows that Phares is troubled, and he's groping for answers," Galen said. "What does the Bible say? *The guilty flee when no man pursueth.*"

"Yes," the preacher said. He was silent. Galen looked at the flat face, the little nose, the small brown eyes.

"He's obviously hiding something, isn't he?" Galen insisted.

Richter wheeled his chair around. "I noticed two things last week. I haven't told a soul. I knew Phares is superstitious, so—"

"What did you see?" Galen asked.

"Did you hear the bell last Wednesday night—the prayer meeting bell?"

"Last Wednesday—oh, the time it rang so loud. Yes, I heard it. It sounded like somebody was pounding on it with a sledge hammer."

"A lot of people noticed it," Richter said. "They said they thought the clapper would fly out of the bell."

Galen leaned forward.

"Well, I went over to the church," the preacher said, "about a half hour before meeting time. Phares usually rings the bell about that time, and he hadn't done it yet. I thought I might have to ring it myself. I went in the church and there was Phares staring wild-eyed at the bell rope. I watched him a few minutes without his noticing me. I never saw anybody look so scared. Finally, I walked up to him and said, 'Well, Phares, it's past time to ring the bell; why don't you ring it?' and he never looked at me; he just kept staring at the rope, and he said in a low voice, 'Jonas will ring it,' and I said, 'Don't talk funny; Jonas is dead; how can he ring the bell?' I went over and shook the rope then and said, 'Look, there's no one here.' He looked at my hands for a minute and then he said, 'Yes, Reverend,' and he took the rope and pulled on it as if he wanted to pull the bell down."

Galen shook his head.

"Then on Thursday morning," Richter said, "I was sitting here at the desk and I saw Phares carry several big flat rocks out and lay them on Jonas' grave. Next time you go past, look at them. You and I together couldn't lift one of those rocks."

"And you think this is natural?"

The preacher was silent.

"Reverend Richter, you know as well as I do that this is the way a guilty man would act. What do we gain by pretending there's no problem? Just as sure as we're sitting here, Phares is afraid. He knows we suspect him. Kenneth is in danger. That's enough reason to do something. I'm not even talking about moral obligation. I'm talking about that child's physical danger. And maybe Chet's, who knows?"

Reverend Richter remained silent. He turned his palms up. "What can we do?"

"Talk to Phares. He's tried to read the Bible; he goes to the Goat Woman—he may be looking for understanding—for redemption—or salvation—or relief—or assurance—or whatever it is that he thinks a man of God could give him."

Richter's face clouded.

"I couldn't meddle like that in people's affairs." He shook his head. "No, Galen, I'm a preacher, not a detective. It's my duty to preach the Gospel. I don't know how things are with Phares's soul. I think they may not be so good. If he comes to me for help in finding God, I'll do what I can. If that would enable him to confess his sins, that would be wonderful—the same is true for this whole town. But you, Galen, you want to put the cart before the horse. You want me to take God to Phares. I'm afraid it works the other way around." Richter smiled. "After all, there's more joy in heaven over one repentant sinner than . . ."

Galen rose. "And, I guess, a great deal of joy in hell over one cowardly angel."

The preacher blinked. He stood up, put his hand on Galen's shoulder, and smiled. "Just remember, Galen, that *though the wrong seems oft so strong, God is the ruler yet.*"

Galen walked stiffly down the stairs, got his jacket and cap, then turned to Richter. "Well, we'll *pray* about it; you'll go along with that, won't you?"

The preacher nodded.

"We'll pray," Galen said, "that God will not permit Phares to add the least of us—a child—to his list."

Richter opened the door, smiling. "Let's add to that," he said, "that if the list is extended it won't be as a result of careless prying or overcuriosity. *There is no ceiling on God's love.*"

"Damn it, Richter," Galen said, "you roll that out as if it means something. Do you mean to say that we don't have to do *anything?* Just what the hell do you think you're saying?"

"Faith is without end, Galen," the preacher said and closed the door.

Galen walked away as fast as he could.

9

"How many saw the movie?" Galen said. Over half the class raised their hands. Kenneth Zercher did not have his hand up. He sat still, looking at his desk.

"Tell me, Christian," Galen said to Crist Bixler, "did you like the movie?"

Crist bobbed his head. "Oh, yes, Mr. Herr; it was *very* exciting."

"For the benefit of those who didn't get to see it, can you give us a quick rundown of the story?"

Crist stood. "Well, there was this here man; he just got out of the Second World War, and he only had one arm; I guess he got it shot off in the war. Anyway he came to this here little town out west some place. He was looking for somebody, the father of a friend that saved his life somewhere in the war. The only thing was, this friend was a Jap. Well, in this little town out west, the people didn't like Japs too good, on account of the war and all. Anyway this man—Spencer Tracy was the man—wanted to find his Japanese friend's father to tell him something, because the Japanese friend was killed when he saved Spencer Tracy's life. You see, these Japs were American citizens. Well, anyway when Spencer Tracy came to this little town, people acted awful funny and nobody would tell him anything about where the old man was."

Crist paused. Florence Weber raised her hand. Crist launched himself again.

"And the reason they all acted so funny was the old man was dead, and the reason he was dead was one time a gang of tough guys led by this one very tough guy got to drinkin' and they went up to the Jap's house and they set the house on fire and the old man burned to death. Well, the more Spencer Tracy tried to find out just what happened and who done it, the more trouble he got into and he ran into an awful lot of danger trying to find out who the killers were and he kept asking people to help him and they were all afraid to, and he just kept at it, and a lot of the people in the town were ashamed of themselves for bein' so cowardly, but Spencer Tracy finally found out everything, and he was very brave and all and it was very good the whole way through."

Galen smiled. "You covered the essential points very well, Christian. Now, class, let's talk about this. Did the hero do the right thing in this movie?"

The students nodded. "Sure!" Florence Weber said.

"But didn't he stir up the town? Didn't he cause a lot of trouble and worry for people? If he hadn't come, they'd have forgotten it, wouldn't they? It was done with—finished. Didn't he expose a lot of people to unpleasantness by prying around the way he did?"

The students looked puzzled.

"Gosh, Mr. Herr," Bill Lichty said, "these men had done a very bad thing."

"What was so bad about what they did?"

"They killed a man in cold blood for no good reason. Everybody knows you're not supposed to do that."

Kathy Sauder raised her hand. "And they picked on this

man because he was a Japanese. You're not supposed to hate people just because of their nationality or their religion."

"All right," Mr. Herr said. "But was it any of Spencer Tracy's business? He didn't even live in the town; they must have had a sheriff. Somehow, don't you think the villains would have paid the penalty—sooner or later?"

"Oh, no, Mr. Herr," Gloria Ranck said. "They'd have gotten away with it. The whole town was willing to overlook it. And it was right for Spencer Tracy to do what he did. A man must do what he can to fight evil wherever he finds it. You said that yourself, Mr. Herr."

"Suppose a thing like that happened in Fair Hill, would you be like all people in the town of the movie or would you act like the hero?"

"I would do like the hero did," Crist Bixler said.

"Oh, yes, you would," a voice said. "You'd be scared just like me."

"If you know that someone has done something wrong," Galen said, "and you don't turn him in—in other words, you protect him—does that make you in part guilty of his crime?"

A few shook their heads, but most nodded. "My pop says," Bill Lichty said, "if you hold the bag you're as guilty as if you put the chickens in."

"Do any of you know anybody who ever stole anything?"

They looked at one another.

"Do you ever see someone cheat on a test?"

An embarrassed silence. Some students nodded.

"Then why have you never reported to me or the other teachers?"

Silence. Crist Bixler said, "Aw, gee, that's different, Mr. Herr." Everybody laughed.

Galen gave the assignment and waited for the buzzer to end the period.

Florence Weber raised her hand. "Mr. Herr, you've asked a lot of questions, but you haven't told us the answers. What—"

"Will we get a test on this?" Crist Bixler interrupted.

"Yes," Galen said, "you may. You may get a test."

"But you didn't give answers, Mr. Herr," Florence Weber said. The buzzer sounded the end of the period.

A few minutes later, after dismissing his homeroom, Galen was in front of the school climbing into the front seat of Charlie Buch's big, black Cadillac hearse. Charlie, in a soft-brown sport jacket, pushed back his plaid cap.

"I'm glad you can go along, Galen," Charlie said. "Alma hates to see me get this crate greased; she's afraid I might have some fun, but with you along she thinks it's all right."

"I'm glad you waited for me," Galen said. "I'm in a good mood for a ride in a hearse. Besides, there's something I want to talk to you about."

Charlie turned the hearse around at the tennis court. "Well, if it's serious, let's wait till the return trip. Right now I want to enjoy the breeze."

The hearse rolled slowly out of town toward the Forge, heading toward the turnpike.

"You know, Galen," the undertaker said, "I envy you."

Galen laughed. "I'm pleased, but why on earth? You have everything."

"Here it is three-thirty," Charlie said, "and you're finished for the day. You get a week at Christmas and a whole summer to do what you like to do."

"Oh," Galen said. "Maybe you'd like to sit up with me tonight while I grade the papers. You of all people, Charlie; how often do you work? Once in a lifetime?"

"It's not that I work hard; it's that I can't *do* anything. I can't go away—not even for a few hours. I just sit around waiting for people to die. At least you know when you have to do your work. The school closes down in June and you couldn't work if you wanted to. You can go away on camping trips. You can get drunk if you want to."

"Aw, Charlie, ain't it tragic?"

"Listen, Galen. A casket salesman gave me a bottle last Christmas—*last Christmas,* mind you, and all I've had so far is a couple shots—for the cold. I look at that damn bottle sometimes and think I'm gonna drink all of it, and then I look at the clock and I can remember a time I was called at just that hour. I wake up sometimes in the middle of the night and I think, 'Now I'll sneak downstairs while Alma's asleep.' Maybe it's three o'clock—I could polish off the bottle and be back in bed in a half an hour, but I know I'd need another eight hours to sleep it off, and I think of all the times I was called to pick up a body between three o'clock and noon. So I go back to bed and the phone doesn't ring the rest of the night or the next day or the day after that—and I could have gotten drunk. Then I get two in the same day or one every day for three or four days. Why, once I had three bodies in the slumber room at the same time. It's just a lonesome job, Galen."

"But look at the money you make, Charlie; you're loaded—a houseful of antiques, the newest cars. I'll bet that sport jacket cost seventy-five dollars. And all from the slumber room."

Charlie looked at his coat and sniffed. "Eighty-nine on sale. Sure, I make money, but there's no fun in the work. When I used to work as a clerk in the stockyard, before I met Alma and took up her dad's business, I made forty dollars a week, but hell, I had some fun and not just after work hours. We used to laugh, tell jokes, play tricks on each other. Tell me, Galen, you ever see a happy undertaker?"

Galen laughed.

"Look at Jake Kutz; he can run the store, and laugh and gossip at the same time. Will Shirk can cut hair and swear if he wants to. Christ, Galen, I can't even swear. If something goes wrong at a funeral—and it does—I just look solemn. I tell you everybody has fun in his work except an undertaker."

Galen sat back. "Well, this is an exception, isn't it? The day you take the hearse to be serviced; that's part of your work. You're gonna have a beer or two, you have flashy clothes; you're gonna open up the hearse a little on the turnpike, and you've already sworn more in the last ten minutes than Will Shirk does in a week."

"You're right, today's my day. The trouble is I can't get the hearse serviced often enough. Do you know how long it takes to put one thousand miles on a hearse?"

Galen shook his head. "Charlie, for heaven's sake, why did you go into this business?"

Charlie stroked the steering wheel. "I like to work with people," he said.

Charlie pulled the big black wagon up to a stop sign at the foot of Blue Mountain. He raced the engine in neutral and the front end trembled. He turned up a mountain driveway and parked before a rustic log cabin. A sign in front said THE HEALING BENEDICTION TAVERN. They entered. Charlie ordered a beer, got a handful of change for the pinball machine. Galen sipped a ginger ale. Charlie drank another beer and they left.

Soon they were on the cloverleaf of the turnpike entrance. Charlie picked up the ticket from the uniformed attendant. On the double lanes east and west, the trucks were roaring under bridges and across overpasses.

Charlie handed the ticket to Galen. "Read those names, man, Keystone City, Scenic Valley." He headed east into the merging traffic strip and onto the turnpike. "I'd just like to floor this thing and go clear across the state two times. . . . Just think, Galen, the outside world—no more black suits, no more saccharine music, no Alma, no wet handkerchiefs."

"You're the spirit of adventure," Galen said.

"That's what I like to see," Charlie shouted above the roar of the engine. "Lots of colors. Look at those out-of-state licenses—roadside tables, people looking at maps."

Galen leaned back in the seat.

"Well, she ought to be loosened up by now," Charlie said.

He turned his side window down and opened the wing side. Then gradually he opened the accelerator—seventy—eighty, for a mile or two, ninety, the engine hummed—one hundred. The needle hung on the magic number. The wind lifted Charlie's coat, flipped a lapel across his tie. The hearse hugged the inside lane, passing the seventy-mile-per-hour traffic as if it were standing still. Galen, his feet pressed into the floorboards, could see astonished faces in the other cars.

"One hundred and five, Galen; watch it, she'll do even better." Charlie hunched over the wheel.

Galen watched the speedometer tensely. "One hundred and ten, Charlie," he shouted. "That's enough for me. Uncle! Uncle!"

"She'll do better," Charlie yelled. For the next minute the needle swung crazily between one ten and one twenty. Then Charlie began to sing:

> Behold, what manner of love,
> What manner of love,
> The Father has bestowed upon us
> That we-e-*eeee,*
> That we should be called the sons of God.

The Gulf station loomed ahead on the right. Charlie took his foot off the accelerator. The hearse slowed suddenly. At fifty it seemed to be standing still. Charlie flipped the turn signals and braked heavily for exit speed. The hot leviathan stopped smoothly before the lubrication platform.

"The usual," Charlie said. He climbed out and turned the hearse, snapping, sighing, creaking, over to an attendant.

Galen and Charlie walked stiffly into the adjoining Howard Johnson's Restaurant and sat at stools at the counter. "Two double-rich malteds," Charlie called to the waitress. He rubbed his hands and turned to Galen. "Well, now, that was a—"

A hand fell on his shoulder. The two men turned around on the stools to face a tall, helmeted State Trooper.

"Which one was driving the hearse?" he asked.

"I—I was," Charlie said.

The trooper looked at him. "I have a present for you," he said.

"Well . . . uh . . . what . . . ?" Charlie said.

"I marked you down for eighty-five miles per. You won't want to protest it. You'll get the notice in a day or so. It will be a ninety-day suspension of operator's license."

"But I'm an undertaker. What if somebody dies? I'll need to drive."

The trooper looked at him coldly. "This way maybe somebody won't die." He slid the ticket into Charlie's coat pocket, turned, and walked from the room.

On the return trip Charlie was subdued; he nursed the heavy vehicle along at forty miles per hour. The sun had gone down and it was almost dark. The air was colder; the windows were up. Traffic was getting heavier.

"What'll I do if there's a funeral?" Charlie moaned.

"That's easy," Galen said. "I'll drive for you. Nobody will think anything about it."

Charlie grunted. "Boy, what Alma's gonna say."

"You in the mood to talk about *my* subject now?" Galen said.

"Yeh. What the hell."

"It's Phares Zercher and Jonas Burkholder. You've heard the talk. You had a chance to look at the body when you embalmed it. Do you think Jonas had a heart attack?"

"Well, I certainly couldn't see his heart, Galen."

"You know what I mean. If Phares killed him, there'd be some marks. Phares isn't subtle. Just tell me there were no marks; then I'll be satisfied."

"Is that what you want to hear?"

Galen hesitated. "No, I want the truth; I hope the truth will be that there were no marks. Then I'll know that Kenneth is acting the way he is because of grief or something and I can work on getting him over that and forget about the rest."

"Well, then," Charlie said, "I'll tell you the truth. And if you tell anybody I told you I'll say you're a goddamn liar. I think Phares choked Jonas to death."

"Are you sure?"

"I could be wrong."

"But you don't think you are," said Galen. "Was there evidence?"

"I noticed it when I shaved Jonas. There were marks on his throat and neck. I didn't think much of it. Later Alma came down to the preparation room—something she doesn't often do—and told me she heard that Phares killed him. Then I took a good look. I told Alma there were no marks because I didn't want her telling anybody. By Sunday the marks were prominent. Bruises sometimes darken hours after death. I covered them and pulled Jonas' collar a little higher for the viewing."

"Good God, Charlie. You were hiding a crime. Why didn't you notify somebody?"

"Well, I wasn't sure. I did say something to Doc Evans the day after, and he guaranteed me that Jonas died of a heart attack. I told him about the marks and he said he noticed them too and that they were marks Jonas got when he fell into the washline. When I thought things over and remembered how irritable Doc was about it and all and I heard about Chet and Kenneth, I just got more and more certain."

"What were the marks, Charlie?"

"Bruises in front—one each side of his Adam's apple. Scratches in the back of the neck around the hairline. Nails digging in could have done it. I've seen that sort of thing before."

Galen bit his lip.

They drove up the exit ramp over the cloverleaf, and Charlie turned over his ticket and thirty-five cents to the attendant.

"Why didn't you put more pressure on Doc Evans?" Galen said.

Charlie shrugged. "It's not my job to tell a coroner how to run his business. If there had been a bullet hole, I'd have called Doc right away. But there are often bruises on a body, almost any body. I'll tell you something, Galen: this sort of thing happens oftener than you think."

"Murder?"

"Technically, yes," Charlie said. "Strangulation or suffocation, usually infants or old people."

"And this doesn't bother you?"

"Oh, I don't like it."

"You think Phares Zercher choked Jonas?"

"Well, you asked," Charlie said.

"I think he did, too," Galen said. "What are we going to do about it?"

Charlie glanced at Galen. "*We? We,* Galen, aren't going to do anything. I might be crazy enough to get myself killed driving this hearse too fast, but I'm not crazy enough to get myself killed by Phares Zercher, or to have Doc Evans ruin my reputation. Think what Doc Evans could do to me—the only doctor in Fair Hill, sees nearly all people before they die. He tells them, 'Don't have Charlie Buch.' Then where am I? No, Galen, I like you fine. You do what you think you should. But count me out."

"I see," Galen said.

When they drove into Fair Hill, it was dark. They turned down College Avenue to Galen's house.

"I'm sorry," Charlie said.

"What for?" Galen asked, opening the door.

"Maybe I'm sorry you take this affair so seriously." He paused. "And maybe I'm sorry I can't be of more help."

"Oh." Galen started to get out.

"Are you going on?" Charlie said. "You going to keep on with this?"

"I don't know."

Charlie sighed and shook his head. "Well, good luck. You realize what you're up against. To prove it you'll have to get Doc to order exhumation of the body for an autopsy. You know how eager he's going to be to do that. Doc's on the school board. If you embarrass *him,* he won't be likely to be much help to you in your job. And there's Phares. Galen, I like you. I don't want to stick a drainage tube in you."

"O.K.," Galen said, leaning down to close the door.

"Why not let sleeping dogs lie?" Charlie said, racing the engine.

"Is that dog eating at Kenneth asleep?" Galen said. He slammed the door and went into the house.

10

The next afternoon about four o'clock Galen Herr waited for Doc Evans at the post office. People milled around inside the brick building exchanging stories while the mail was sorted. Galen saw the doctor approaching, his arms swinging as he walked. Doc pushed his dark-rimmed glasses up and waved to everybody as he entered the building and went to unlock his box. Galen stepped outside and waited. In a minute Doc came out, riffling a stack of letters.

"Hi, Doc," Galen said. "Do you have a few minutes to talk?"

Doc looked up and smiled. "I have to get back to the house—gotta get a bite to eat and go to Red Rose." He stuck the letters into his coat pocket, took out a package of cigarettes, offered them to Galen, and lit one himself. Galen waited. Doc rubbed the heel of his hand along his right temple. "I'll tell you what, Galen, walk along toward my house. We'll talk on the way."

"Fair enough," Galen said. "I'll come right to the point. It's about Jonas Burkholder. I'm concerned about his death."

"So?" Doc said.

"I'd like to know how he died," Galen said.

"You know how he died," Doc said. "It was in the paper—public information. He died of a coronary." He flicked the ash from his cigarette. "People seem to get a thrill out of asking."

"Maybe they've heard the same story I heard," Galen said.

"Well, it's nonsense," Doc said. "Look, Galen, Kenneth came back for me the day Jonas died. He talked to Mildred. Now, why wouldn't he say something to her? He just said for me to come as soon as possible. Now why do you insist on believing that he ran across the street to Chet Lehman and said that Phares was killing Jonas? Why wouldn't he have said the same thing to Mildred?"

Galen shook his head. "Who knows? Maybe with Chet the boy was scared for Jonas. With Mildred he was scared for himself."

"I think it's about time we all forgot about this thing," Doc said. "Jonas died of a heart attack."

Galen rubbed his crew-cut hair and took a deep breath. "You're *sure?*" He watched the doctor.

Doc stopped. "Yes, I'm sure. What else you want to know?"

"Did you perform an autopsy?"

Doc walked on. "Let's talk about education. How's everything at the school? You know, even though I'm on the school board, I don't meddle in your business. But since you're moving into medicine, maybe I'd better."

"I'm sorry you take it that way," Galen said. "I'm not saying you should have done an autopsy. I trust you. I believe it was a coronary. But can't a coronary be induced?"

"Listen," Doc said, "I knew Jonas' condition. I knew the general direction he was moving. He finally had it. At seventy-six. Is that premature?"

They turned the corner at Broad Street, walked past the town clock.

"You know," Doc said, "Grandma Lesher's going to die one of these days. It may be today, tomorrow, next month, and I won't do an autopsy on her either. It'll be a stroke." They stopped in the slanting driveway beside the Evans house. The upstairs window was open; a blanket was hanging over the sill. "And I won't suspect any foul play there either unless her throat is cut."

Upstairs Suzie Kulp appeared at the window and gathered in the blanket. Galen waited until she was gone. "And there were no such marks on Jonas?" he said.

"Nothing significant—oh, maybe a little bruise Jonas got when he fell into the washline sometime before."

Galen looked at him. "Doc, would you be willing, in view of the stories, would you be willing to order exhumation of Jonas' body? Just to be sure?"

Doc snapped the cigarette butt onto the asphalt. "Galen Herr, you are the most persistent, the most—" Doc stopped. He said, slowly, "Galen, you aren't much younger than I am. Why do you act so damned juvenile? You've been teaching school too long. Why don't you work in the world awhile? You act like a good little schoolboy."

"Maybe I do," Galen said, "but there's a lot involved here. You make the sick well. I teach the ignorant. I'm not a schoolboy; I teach schoolboys; I'm worried about one of my schoolboys. I want him to know the difference between good and evil."

"Don't be so damn sure you can tell good from evil," Doc said. "You're lucky if you can tell it about yourself, much less about other people. You examine yourself. Not me. Not Phares. You tend your business. Teaching books."

Galen smiled. "You and Richter make a good team. He says it's God's business. You say it's not my business. In either case, let the kid suffer. Let him see that nobody cares and nobody helps."

"You're some help," Doc said. "That kid doesn't need an enemy with you for a friend. Now for your own good, you go back and teach verbs and dangling participles, and if you want a cause, pick something like famines in India or the plight of the Navajo, and let's cut out this crap about how you think Jonas died."

Galen looked up over Zimmerman's Hill. Grey clouds rimmed the horizon.

"But if there were specific evidence in this case—specific evidence, testimony. Then you'd have to dig up the body, wouldn't you?"

"Get it and see," Doc said. He turned abruptly toward the door. Galen sighed and started out Broad Street.

11

By seven o'clock Suzie was in the sexton's kitchen. She flattened her buttocks against the dry sink, folded her arms under her bosom, and watched Phares pace back and forth in front of the stove.

"I told you last week already," he said hoarsely. "I gotta finish Doc Evans." His eyes were bloodshot; his shoulders hung forward, and he kept clenching and unclenching his right hand. "I mighta knowed it right in the beginning."

"Shh, Phares, not so loud," Suzie whispered, and made a motion with her head toward the door to the stairway leading to Kenneth's room. "Now be quiet once and listen to me. I told you Doc ain't gonna dig up the body. He don't want to. You just don't see *anything* straight any more."

The big vein stood out on Phares's forehead. "But he's the one that could dig up the body if he wanted to; you said that. Nobody else can make one of them—whatever you call it."

"Autopsy."

"Yes, Doc's the one to do that, and he *will* do it if I don't do something."

"Stop it," Suzie said. She came near. "I thought you were a strong man. I tell you Doc Evans is nothing to be afraid of. It's the schoolteacher that's stickin' his nose in. . . ."

"Yes, well, I can fix him, too. It doesn't matter now anyhow. Nothing works out the way I want it. They always say if you have blood on one hand you will get it on the other."

"That isn't necessary, Phares; now you listen to me." Suzie took his nervously clenching right hand. Phares shook free.

"I listened to you too much already. If I wouldn't of listened to you I wouldn't be where I am now."

Suzie flushed. "That's not right, Phares. You made a *doplich* mistake. Right in the beginning you left your temper get the best of you."

"Well, I can't stand it, Suzie," Phares hissed between clenched teeth. "I can't stand to wait around and look at everybody and half the time I don't know what they're up to. Why don't they come in here–" he clenched his hands behind his back. "Why don't they get Milt Frey and the whole damn town, that *fadumpti* schoolteacher, and every man in Fair Hill and come in here after me." He shook his fist at the door. "Leave 'em come in oncet; chust let 'em all come in here oncet and say, 'You killed Jonas.' Leave them say that to my face and I'll kill all them sons-of-bitches."

"Not so loud, Phares; not so loud." Suzie stood in front of him. "I know, you want to break things and tramp on things, but that's no help now. If you do that, *you'll* be finished. You take it easy. Do with Galen Herr a little like you done with Chet Lehman. There's no trouble with Chet any more, is there? Well, just leave the teacher know you mean business."

"Ach, I'm tired of chust makin' like I mean business. I'm chust gonna go down there and knock his head in–and then I'll get that doctor and I don't care what happens."

Suzie walked over to Phares, put her arms around his waist, and pressed herself to him.

"Calm down, Phares, and be a little more the way you used to be. You must care what happens."

Phares relaxed and put his hands on Suzie's shoulder.

"Watch for a good chance," Suzie said. "The teacher walks up through the cemetery almost every day. Go meet him and keep your temper. But tell him you know he's been minding your business and if he don't stop right away you're gonna make him sorry."

Phares nodded his head.

"You know, Phares, there's more than one way to scare a body. You don't always have to beat somebody up. Look at you; there ain't anybody in Red Rose County could lick you; yet you're afraid of a lot of things. Now what do you think might work with the schoolteacher?"

Phares thought. "Suzie, I'm scared."

"He has two little boys, Phares," Suzie said. "And his wife's big as a house again." Phares's eyes lighted. "He likes his family, Phares; he plays with those boys; they go camping together in the summer. Just tell him something bad will happen to them; that'll stop him."

Phares stretched to his full height, dropped his hands to his belt. "I don't know if I can do that. When I walk up to people I get mad; I chust want to tear them apart. But if you're sure it will work and then people won't look at me like I was a dog?"

Suzie put her arms around his neck and pulled him down to kiss her.

"You try, Phares." She took his right hand and pressed it against her breast. "I think now this would be a good time to go over to our room in the basement."

Phares stared over her shoulder. "I don't know if it would."

Suzie rubbed her body against him. "I'll go over first and get ready for you," she whispered.

"Maybe we should wait."

"Why wait?" she said. "Wait for what?"

"Until I talk to the teacher; then I could tell how your idea will work."

Suzie's hands caressed him. "I'll leave in a few minutes, Phares. And I'll go over to our room and I'll take all my clothes off and I'll wait for you there." She drew away from him. "You wait about fifteen minutes and think about me over there on the cot. Think hard, Phares, all that time and then come over." She opened the door and then paused. "I need you, Phares. You are a *man*, Phares."

She closed the door behind her; Phares stood motionless a moment, staring; then he walked to the range and held his hands over the warmth, looking at the black lids. Suddenly he turned and picked up Jonas' German Bible. He opened it at random, read. He closed it; opened it, and read again. He shut it, and sank into a chair.

Several minutes later he turned out the kitchen light, opened the door, and stepped out into the night. He examined the sky, sniffed the air, then walked behind the house and toward the church. Standing between the two buildings, he could see Main Street from the post office down to the street light at Union Street. He stood, looking at the empty street.

A form emerged from the school alley onto Main Street. It walked hurriedly across the street under the street light and on down toward Frog Hollow. Phares recognized the familiar cap and jacket and his nostrils flared. The figure turned left into the alley that ran between Union and Broad.

The shadowy figure disappeared behind garages and outhouses and appeared again at the back gate of the Lehman property.

12

Galen Herr paused at the gate. Main Street seemed deserted. There were no lights across the street at the sexton's cottage. So far so good. The smells from the Lehman outhouse and garbage pile filled the air. Washline posts and tangled rotting vines clotted in the darkness. The back yards were all alike—pump beds, washlines, flagstone walks, toilets, sheds. A back door slammed. A dog barked suddenly several houses away.

Galen walked up the back path quickly, onto the porch to the kitchen door. Chester Lehman was reading the newspaper at the table beneath the light of a sixty-watt bulb. Galen tapped on the pane and Chet jumped as if he had been hit by a charge of electricity. Galen pressed his face against the pane. Chet came to the door, turned the key, and let Galen into the kitchen.

A low fire in the range warmed the room. The linoleum was spotless. An apothecary jar filled with pink mints stood in the center of the table.

"I'm sorry to break in on you like this," Galen said, "but I have to talk with you."

Chet reddened. "It's just that I'm a little jumpy lately."

"That's why you keep the door locked?"

"Nellie locked it when she went to bed," Chet said.

"I don't blame you," Galen said. "It won't be long before everybody in Fair Hill will be locking doors."

"What do you mean by that?"

"An old man was murdered; the man who did it can't feel safe."

"Don't come here," Chet said. He opened the icebox. "Don't say things to me." He closed the icebox. "You don't have anything to do with me."

"You had a visit from Phares," Galen said.

Chet sat down. "How did you know that?"

"It's obvious," Galen said.

"Please," Chet said, "what do you want from me?" He looked away.

"That won't do you any good," Galen said. "Everybody knows Phares has you scared."

"There is nothing to do," Chet said, rubbing his hands and staring at the stove. "You want me to leave Fair Hill?"

"That makes sense, but we can't all leave," Galen said. "If it's true, there is only one thing to do, prove that Phares killed Jonas and have him brought to trial. If you just told the State Troopers what happened that day, they would arrest Phares."

Chet shook his head rapidly. "I don't know anything." He rose. "It's crazy. Phares said he'd kill me and he *would*."

"We could get protection," Galen said. "There's more danger in the long run if we don't."

Chet's head was still shaking. "No," he said. "No."

"If you're unwilling to do it yourself, at least tell me that you will give the truth to a State Trooper if *I* call one in."

"What?"

"Look, I'll go to the police. You just stay in the house. I'll tell them that on a certain day Kenneth Zercher ran across the street to you and asked you to help, that his father was killing Jonas. That much is true, isn't it?"

Chet shook his head. "No. No. Kenneth said Phares was shaking him, maybe hurting him, he didn't say killing. But you don't need *me*. Get Kenneth to say what happened. He saw." Chet brightened. "You don't really need me at all. What good would it be if I said one thing and Kenneth said another thing? But if Kenneth would tell the truth, then it wouldn't matter what I said. Ain't that right?"

Galen sighed. "All right, Chet." He rose. "But that isn't the way Phares thinks. You better take care of yourself."

Chet looked at the window.

Galen left by the back door. He crossed the back porch, stepped down the four wooden steps to the walk, and went toward the alley. The night was still the same, perhaps a bit brighter with a few more stars. There seemed to be more cars on Main Street. He slid the crossbar on the gate and stepped into the gravel surface of the alley. He walked into the shadow of a garage. A hand grabbed his shoulder and spun him around. Before he could get his hands up, a blow struck him in the face. He lurched; a heavy fist slammed into his ribs. Breath left his body. His face shocked again; pain sliced into his eyes. He fell. He lay there; then he was jerked to his feet.

"All right, schoolteacher. I'll teach *you* something." He could see the bearded face inches from his eyes. He could smell the big man's breath. "I should kill you right here, you goddam meddler." Then Galen was flung through the air. He landed sitting, and rolled over. The bearded face was over him. "Now I tell you something, schoolteacher; keep your nose out of my business. The next time I'll go for those two boys of yours and that knocked-up wife of yours." He shook Galen violently. "How would you like to come sometime and find them on the garbage pile?"

"They—" Galen gasped. "No, Phares—"

"I'll be watching you; you will see what I can do. Now get out of here." He spun Galen around and pushed him down the alley. Galen lurched in the direction of Union Street.

His nose felt crunched and huge. His face was hot and swollen. "You yellow son-of-a-bitch," he whispered. "You spineless bastard."

His face was wet.

"Cry, you goddam baby," he said. He stumbled, and began to run.

13

Three o'clock the next afternoon, Galen, in pajamas and robe, sat by the kitchen window, looking across the cemetery. A bruise the color of the church window was under his right eye. A brush burn scraped his right cheek. His mouth was split and puffed. Anna brought a cup to him.

"Can you manage a little broth?" she asked.

Galen worked his lips and probed the inside of his mouth with his tongue. "I think I can," he said. He felt his jaw. "I think he loosened every tooth in my head."

"You're looking a little better by the hour; thank heavens for that." She wiped her hands on an apron that stood out over her swollen stomach. She ran her fingers through his stubby hair and then walked back to the stove.

"I feel pretty good," Galen said. "I should have gone to school."

"That's ridiculous," Anna said, pushing the unruly lock of hair out of her eye. "You were in no condition this morning. Besides, it's better if people don't go around wondering who beat you up."

There was a scurrying along the hall, and Buck and Butch came into the kitchen.

"Can we play outside now, Mom?" Butch said.

"No, you can't," Anna said. "Now go on upstairs and stay in your room." She glanced at Galen.

"Aw, gee, Mommy," Buck said. "Why, Mommy?"

"Because it's . . . it's too cold; you have plenty of games to play in your room."

"But it was colder than this yesterday, Mom," Butch protested. "You never made us stay in before."

She looked at Galen again. He nodded.

"All right," she said, with a sigh. "You can play here in the side yard." The boys jumped and shouted. "But if you leave the side yard I'll make you come in." The boys scrambled for their coats, and dashed out the door.

Anna came back and sat in a chair beside Galen. "What are we going to do?"

Galen patted her knee. "You're a good woman."

"Yeah, I'm a good woman; if something happens to those boys I'll feel like a great woman. What are we going to do, Galen?"

Galen sipped some broth. "Well, we keep calm, and we keep our eyes open." He nodded toward the closet. "We have a twelve-gauge double-barreled shotgun and a box of shells. You can hit a clay target, you can hit a big man with it. It's broad daylight; it's our back yard. He's not going to come down here and do anything. He just wants to scare me off this thing. You and the boys stay in at night anyhow and I'll stay with you. We'll see how he reacts if he thinks he's scared me away. If he calms down, comes back to normal—well, we'll forget it. But if he gets worse and worse and we all have to be more afraid even than we are now, then I'll pack you off to your sister's in Red Rose."

"Then you've decided to stop playing secret investigator?"

Galen shrugged.

"Well, it's welcome news to me," she said. "You *have* done your part, you know. I admire your sense of duty or whatever it is, but it's enough." She leaned over and kissed him on the bruised cheek. "So let it be, please."

Galen got up stiffly. "I wouldn't quit if I could think of anything else to do. Nobody else will help. Charlie Buch's afraid he may lose business if he alienates Doc. Richter's afraid he'll be tampering with God's plan. Doc doesn't think you can right a wrong no matter how hard you try; Chet's scared silly; Kenneth is stunned. And everybody is scared of Phares and the truth." Galen spread his hands. "Without the help of at least one of them, I'm licked."

"Maybe the Goat Woman?" Anna said, unwillingly.

Galen snorted. "No, thanks. I don't want to mess with the instruments of darkness."

Anna looked at him. "What's that: instruments of darkness? Did you make it up?"

Galen raised his eyebrows. "It just popped into my mind. It's from Shakespeare, I think. Somebody said it in *Macbeth*—Banquo, I think. 'But 'tis strange and oftentimes to win us to our harm the instruments of darkness tell us truths, win us with honest trifles to betray us in deepest consequence.' He was talking about witches."

"Oh," Anna said. She pulled herself out of the chair. "I think I'll clean the living room."

She left the kitchen and Galen sipped the broth. Fall colors were calm in the valley. Husked corn lay in yellow heaps. Stalks stood in brown shocks. The words of Jonas' poem came into Galen's mind. *My Valley, white in winter, green in spring, and gold in summer's long, limp days. . . .*

"Now faded into fall," Galen said. He sat, rested, watching colors flickering and softening as clouds moved over the sun.

Then he saw a movement in the cemetery. It was Phares Zercher—carrying a basket of debris. Phares walked to the southern end of the cemetery, turned west, skirting Jonas' grave, and dumped his load in the cut. He stood there, turned and walked back toward the church, the basket swinging beside him.

Galen watched the long firm strides, the big hands swinging —hangman's hands, Galen thought. He counted the steps—one, two, three—the words passed through his mind—"With Tarquin's ravishing strides." Galen watched Phares walk along the southern edge to the driveway, then up toward Main Street, *with Tarquin's ravishing strides.* Then the other lines came into his mind: *Now o'er the one half-world Nature seems dead, and wicked dreams abuse the curtain'd sleep; witchcraft celebrates pale Hecate's offerings; and wither'd murther, alarum'd by his sentinel, the wolf, whose howl's his watch, thus with his stealthy pace, with Tarquin's ravishing strides, toward his design moves like a ghost.*

Galen rose. "Anna, Anna," he said, "come here!" Anna dropped her dust cloth and came toward him. "The boys?" she gasped.

"It's not the boys," Galen said. "It's an idea. Come and listen."

Anna sighed. "You scared me half to death."

"I was watching Phares walk up through the cemetery," Galen said. "It just came to me how much like Macbeth he is."

Anna raised her eyebrows.

"Don't you see? He's a big strong man; he murdered an old man to take over his house and his job; he sees the Goat Woman; he believes in ghosts—"

"I don't remember," Anna said. "It's been some time since I read Shakespeare."

"It's fresh in my mind," Galen said. "I can't see why I didn't think of it before. We read the play earlier in the fall, and I never saw the connection."

Anna frowned, "So, does it help you any? You believe now?"

"It's a way to get to Kenneth," Galen said. "Do you remember I told you how I heard Kenneth sobbing when I knocked on the door the Saturday Jonas died—was killed? Phares scolded Kenneth for going to pieces every time someone knocked on the door."

Anna cocked her head and looked at Galen out of the corner of her eye. "I still don't see—"

"Then," Galen said:

> *Be innocent of the knowledge, dearest chuck,*
> *Till thou applaud the deed.*

"Aw, nuts," Anna said.

14

Galen held up the book.

The class looked.

"The first time we read a book," Galen said, "we want to know *what happened.* We're curious. We rush forward in the story to find out what happens next. But after we know what happened, we can rest, we can go back and move slowly, quietly through the story and find out something more important. We want to know *why* it happened.

"Today we will go back over *Macbeth.* We will discover that there is no end to the meaning of a work of art. We will find new relationships. Perhaps—and maybe this is the best pleasure of all—we will discover that we know more than we think we know."

Gertrude Schaeffer raised her hand.

"Yes?" Galen said.

"Mister Herr," she said, "that story's simple. It's about ambition. Macbeth was so ambitious he killed a man and got punished."

"Well," Galen said, "you're right. He killed a man out of ambition. And he suffered for that act. But now where did the suffering come from? Did Macbeth suffer most from what others did to punish him?"

"Sure," Crist Bixler said. "After Macbeth got all he wanted, they went and took it away from him—and killed him."

Florence Weber waved. Galen nodded.

"No!" she said. "Macbeth suffered from guilt. And Lady Macbeth too. They were always talking about their hands."

"Yes," Galen said. "You mean they punished themselves more than anybody else could punish them?"

"Yes," Florence said. "They knew they did wrong."

Galen laughed. "You mean to tell me that they didn't know it was wrong *before* they did it?"

Florence opened her mouth. She shook her head.

Kenneth twisted in his seat, his elbow striking the desk.

"Kenneth?" Galen said.

Kenneth looked up quickly. "I didn't . . . I didn't put up my hand, sir."

"I know," Galen said. He waited.

Kenneth pressed one hand over the other on the desk top. "It was only an idea," he said.

"What was?" Galen said.

"Before they did it, it was only an idea," Kenneth said.

"Good," Galen said. "Before it was an act, it was only an idea. An idea can be changed, can be evaporated. But when the idea becomes an act—becomes a thing—it cannot evaporate. Who said it—was it Lady Macbeth?—*What is done cannot be undone?*"

"That's right," Florence said. "They felt guilty."

"Well," Galen said, "let's see if we can understand more about that. Who can give us a quick summary of the first act?"

Gertrude Schaeffer waved and stood. "There was a battle," she said. "Macbeth and Banquo were brave generals fighting for King Duncan, and there were three witches that planned to see them after the battle. Well, the witches did see them on the heath—you said that was a big field sorta—and the witches told Macbeth that he would be king some day, and they also called him the *thane* of something."

"Thane of Glamis," Crist Bixler said.

"Thane of Cawdor," Kathy Sauder said.

"Yes," Galen said. "Thane is a Scottish rank—or was—something like an English earl. Macbeth was Thane of Glamis. That was his father's title before him, but how did he react to being called Thane of Cawdor, and to the prophecy that he would become king?"

Gertrude shook her head. Hands went up.

"Bill," Galen said.

"He didn't believe it," Bill Lichty said. "He said that the present Thane of Cawdor was still alive, and he just couldn't believe that he would be king."

"And then?"

"Right after that," Bill said, "some men come in and they say that the Thane of Cawdor was a traitor and that Duncan had him executed and that Duncan was giving the title to Macbeth. And this news makes Macbeth think the witches know what they are talking about, and he figures if they knew he was going to be Thane of Cawdor, they're maybe right about the king part too. So he starts to think about ways he can get to be king, and he writes a letter to Lady Macbeth, and she's all excited about it. She really wants to be queen, I guess, because she wants Macbeth to hurry home so she can talk him into—murdering, I guess—Duncan. Well, about the time Macbeth got home, here comes a messenger all out of breath and says that Duncan is coming to pay a visit. And she thinks, 'Oh, boy, here's our chance.' Then she goes to work on Macbeth."

"Slow down, Bill," Galen said. "You're almost as much out of breath as the messenger."

"Well, Macbeth about half doesn't wanta do it, and she gets burned up at him—and they're so nice to Duncan it almost makes you sick—and she keeps nagging at Macbeth, and finally he says he'll do it. And I believe that's the end of the first act." Bill sat down.

"Good," Galen said. "Good. Now, let's examine the work itself. The first scene of the second act is the court of Macbeth's castle. Banquo and Fleance have some conversation, you remember, that makes us expect the coming crime; then Banquo and Macbeth talk about the three witches. At last Macbeth is alone." Galen put the book down. "Shall we act it out?"

Heads nodded.

"All right," Galen said. "Kathy, you read the part of Lady Macbeth. And I'll do the sound effects. And for Macbeth, himself—let's see—Kenneth, you read."

Kenneth rubbed his forehead. He and Kathy Sauder came forward.

"All right," Galen said. "Macbeth is about to go to the bedroom to kill Duncan. It's hard for him to do. Now read with feeling."

Kenneth began, his voice uncertain:

> Is this a dagger which I see before me,
> The handle toward my hand? Come let me clutch thee:
> I have thee not, and yet I see thee still.
> Art thou not, fatal vision, sensible
> To feeling as to sight? or art thou but
> A dagger of the mind, a false creation,
> Proceeding from the heat-oppressed brain?

The students leaned forward. Kenneth read on, his voice wavering.

> . . . Now o'er the one half-world
> Nature seems dead, and wicked dreams abuse
> The curtain'd sleep! witchcraft celebrates
> Pale Hecate's offerings, and wither'd murther,
> Alarum'd by his sentinel, the wolf,
> Whose howl's his watch, thus with his stealthy pace,
> With Tarquin's ravishing strides, toward his design

Moves like a ghost. Thou sure and firm-set earth,
Hear not my steps, which way they walk, for fear
Thy very stones prate of my whereabout,
And take the present horror from the time,
Which now suits with it. Whiles I threat, he lives:
Words to the heat of deeds too cold breath gives.
I go, and it is done. The bell invites me.
Hear it not, Duncan, for it is a knell
That summons thee to heaven, or to hell.

Galen interrupted. "Now we see Lady Macbeth waiting for Macbeth to come back with the news that he has killed Duncan. She has drugged the guards; she knows that he has a good chance to do the deed, but then she hears a noise, and she is afraid somebody may have awakened. Then Macbeth returns with the daggers; she greets him with the words, 'My husband!' Go ahead, Kenneth. You answer, Kathy."

"I have done the deed," Kenneth read. "Didst thou not hear a noise?"

KATHY: I heard the owl scream and the crickets cry.
Did not you speak?
KENNETH: When?
KATHY: Now.
KENNETH: As I descended?
KATHY: Ay.
KENNETH: Hark! Who lies i' th' second chamber?
KATHY: Donalbain.
KENNETH: This is a sorry sight.
KATHY: A foolish thought to say a sorry sight.
KENNETH: There's one did laugh in's sleep, and one cried 'Murther!'
That they did wake each other. I stood and heard them.
But they did say their prayers, and address'd them
Again to sleep.
KATHY: There are two lodg'd together.
KENNETH: One cried 'God bless us!' and 'Amen' the other:
As they had seen me with these hangman's hands.

List'ning their fear, I could not say 'Amen!'
When they did say 'God bless us!'

KATHY: Consider it not so deeply.

KENNETH: But wherefore could I not pronounce 'Amen'?
I had most need of blessing, and 'Amen'
Stuck in my throat.

KATHY: These deeds must not be thought
After these ways. So, it will make us mad.

KENNETH: Methought I heard a voice cry 'Sleep no more!
Macbeth does murther sleep.'—the innocent sleep,
Sleep that knits up the ravell'd sleave of care,
The death of each day's life, sore labour's bath,
Balm of hurt minds, great nature's second course,
Chief nourisher in life's feast.

KATHY: What do you mean?

KENNETH: Still it cried 'Sleep no more!' to all the house;
"Glamis hath murther'd sleep, and therefore Cawdor
Shall sleep no more! Macbeth shall sleep no more!"

KATHY: Who was it that thus cried? Why, worthy Thane,
You do unbend your noble strength to think
So brainsickly of things. Go get some water
And wash this filthy witness from your hand.
Why did you bring these daggers from the place?
They must lie there; go carry them and smear
The sleepy grooms with blood.

KENNETH: I'll go no more.
I am afraid to think what I have done;
Look on't again I dare not.

Kenneth's voice was low. His eyes were on the book and his lips twitched.

Kathy answered:

Infirm of purpose!
Give me the daggers. The sleeping and the dead
Are but as pictures. 'Tis the eye of childhood
That fears a painted devil. If he do bleed,

> I'll gild the faces of the grooms withal,
> For it must seem their guilt.

Galen knocked on the desk lightly. Kenneth looked up from his book. He paled.

"Whence is that knocking?" he faltered. "How is't with me when every noise appals me? What hands are here? Ha! they pluck out mine eyes. Will all great Neptune's ocean wash this blood clean from my hand? No. This my hand will rather the multitudinous seas incarnadine, making the green one red."

Kathy answered: "My hands are of your colour, but I shame to wear a heart so white."

Galen knocked again on the desk, louder.

"I hear a knocking at the south entry," Kathy said. "Retire we to our chamber. A little water clears us of this deed. How easy it is then! Your constancy hath left you unattended."

Galen knocked still louder. Kenneth licked his lips and swayed.

"Hark! more knocking," Kathy said. "Get on your nightgown, lest occasion call us, and show us to be watchers. Be not lost so poorly in your thoughts."

Kenneth took a deep breath. He read quickly, loudly: "To know my deed, 'twere best not to know myself."

Galen banged the desk with his fist.

Kenneth shouted, "Wake Duncan with thy knocking!" The book fell to the floor. "I would thou couldst!"

He ran to the door leading into the next room, and fumbled at the knob. The door slammed behind him.

"All right," Galen said. "All right. We'll dismiss early today. File out quietly, please. We'll continue *Macbeth* tomorrow."

He sat at the desk and watched the students leave.

Finally, he arose and went through the door into the chemistry laboratory.

Kenneth sat on a stool by the sinks. He stared at the gas jet.

Galen sat down on the next stool.

"I'm sorry, Mr. Herr," Kenneth said.

"That's all right," Galen said.

Kenneth was silent. He leaned on the bar, his hands trembling. He reached out and turned on the gas jet. Gas hissed.

Galen turned it off.

"It's *not* all right," Kenneth said. "It won't *ever* be."

Galen sat, still.

"It's an ugly play," he said.

"It's not the play." Kenneth covered his face with his hand. "It's not the play." He put his head down on his hands.

"It's your Uncle Jonas, isn't it?" Galen said.

"I miss him." His voice was muffled. "I miss him."

"Well," Galen said. "He was a wonderful man. But he *was* old, Kenneth."

"He didn't have to," Kenneth said. "He didn't have to die."

Galen didn't move. Kenneth lifted his head and looked at Galen.

"Your father?" Galen said.

Kenneth's eyes widened.

"Kenneth," Galen said, "life has no meaning if we don't do what is right. It costs terribly to do what is right. But it costs more not to do what is right."

"I don't *know* what's right," Kenneth cried.

"The truth is right," Galen said. "Trust in the truth. There is no other way to decide."

Kenneth moaned.

"Just tell the truth," Galen said. "Don't blame anybody. Don't hate anybody. Don't fear anybody. Just tell the truth, Kenneth."

Muscles worked in the boy's face.

"What happened the day Jonas died?"

The boy turned away.

Galen touched Kenneth's shoulder. "Your father is suffering too. He is suffering, too, Kenneth. He needs to be helped. As you need help. The truth will help, Kenneth. Your father in his suffering may do more things, worse things."

The boy quivered.

"You know it, Kenneth. He needs help."

The boy stared at Galen. "He shook him," he said. "Father shook Uncle Jonas. His head was like his neck was broken!"

"Did you tell Chet Lehman, 'I think Father will kill Jonas'?"

"No!" the boy said. "I never said that. I said maybe Father is shaking Jonas or hurting Jonas. I didn't say *kill*."

"And then Jonas *was* dead?"

"Yes." The boy sobbed loudly. "Yes."

"All right," Galen said. He kept his hand on the boy's shoulder. "You're doing right. Now you relax. Don't go home. I'm going to call and make arrangements."

He led the boy back to the silent classroom.

15

Phares sat at the kitchen table. Open before him was Jonas' old German Bible. He read the title page: "*Die Bibel. Die ganze Heilige Schrift.*"

He closed the book, heavy fingers resting on the embossed leather cover. "The holy writings," he said. "If I could understand chust oncet. Chust oncet." He placed both hands on the book.

The door flung open.

Phares hurled himself from the table and swung around.

Suzie Kulp stood, breathless, her breasts still swinging. "Phares," she said, "Phares."

Phares shook his fists. "*Gut fadumpsi,*" he said. "Don't bust in! I told you before don't bust in!"

"Phares," Suzie said, "I got to tell you."

"Always you tell me," Phares said. "Leave me alone oncet. You already give me enough trouble. Don't tell me any more."

"Phares," Suzie said.

"Look." Phares pointed to a crumpled paper on the table. "Now I get from the school a note. Kenneth got sick; they took him to the hospital. They don't tell me what's wrong. Is he bad sick? I'm a father; they don't tell me."

"Oh, he's not sick," Suzie said.

"And how about if Kenneth talks in his sleep again? If he talks *there?* What will happen?"

"Be quiet!" Suzie said. "Listen to me. I was making supper at Doc Evans' house. From the kitchen I heard them talk. Listen—"

"Listen to some more of your ideas about how I should do? You shut up. I don't want to hear. Jonas is dead. Where is it what I did it for? You made it sound so good. It took me half a hour longer today to dig Grandma Lesher's grave. What I eat don't go to my muscles no more. I chust think all the time, 'Where is this life Suzie talked about?' "

"I heard Doc and Mildred talk, Phares," Suzie said. "He said he's going to order Jonas' body dug up."

"What?" Phares said.

"Kenneth isn't in the hospital. He's in the Children's Shelter in Red Rose. He told the schoolteacher."

"Kenneth told," Phares said.

"The schoolteacher told Doc. They're going to the police."

Phares stepped toward Suzie. "Why in the hell didn't you tell me right away? Why do you keep this from me?"

"I finished supper, Phares," Suzie said. "Then I came right away. They would think it funny if I ran out in the middle of serving supper."

"That schoolteacher," Phares said. "Doc Evans. I am like a dog to them. Like a goddamned dog."

"Well," Suzie said. "They'll dig up Jonas and find out Kenneth told the truth. They will come for you, Phares."

"I am not a goddamned dog," Phares said. "I got rights."

Suzie put her hand on the doorknob. "I done my part. I told you and you wouldn't listen. If I would be in your shoes, Phares, I'd go hide right away. I have to go back now."

Phares moved. His hand closed over her hand on the knob.

"*I* should go hide? They will come for *me?* Suzie, they will come for *us,* won't they? Where shall we go?"

Suzie pulled at the knob. "Phares, you did it. If I ran away, it would look like I did it, too. You go, Phares. You take care of yourself."

Phares took her by the shoulders. "You talked, you talked." His thumbs pressed into her flesh. "Day and night you talked. I wouldn't a done it." He shook her. "I wouldn't a *never* done it."

"You're hurting me, Phares." She pushed his chest. "Now stop."

Phares stared. "You are like that Goat Woman. You get me in this fix and you want to leave me. No! You will not do it. You will not. You chust will not. You evil bitch."

Suzie looked at him, her body rigid. She began to squirm. His hands pressed deeper and he shook her slowly and then more quickly.

"No," she said. Her head snapped back and forth. She screamed and Phares let go of her shoulders and seized her neck.

The scream choked off.

His hands relaxed. Suzie gasped in air. She began again, a high thin scream. His hands tightened. In the silence, Suzie's face flushed.

Phares looked. Suzie's face was red. His hands locked. Her face darkened. He held. She twisted and scratched and kicked. He lifted her free of the floor. Her face was blood purple. She hung slack.

He stared, lowered the body, and laid it on the floor.

He stood by the table and the leather Bible. He reached and opened the book. *Das andere Buch Mose. Das 32.Capitel.* He held the page down. The German words began, heavy in the tiny kitchen.

"Und er sprach zu ihnen," Phares said. *"So spricht der Herr, der Gott Israels: Gürte ein Jeglicher sein Schwerdt auf seine*

Lenden, und durchgehet hin und wieder, von einem Thor zum andern im Lager, und erwürge ein Jeglicher seinen Bruder, Freund und Nächsten."

Phares stood, his head nodding. "Yes, by God! Every man put on a sword. Go from gate to gate. And kill. Brother, Friend, Neighbor. I understand it. Until all are clean. That is what a man does."

He closed the book, his hand light on the leather-bossed *Die Bibel oder die ganze Heilige Schrift.*

16

Galen returned from Red Rose near midnight. A light was in the kitchen. Anna unlocked and opened the door as he crossed the porch.

"Where in the world have you been?" she asked. "I was beginning to imagine all kinds of things."

"The boys asleep?" Galen said.

"Yes, but they cut up awhile."

Galen hung up his hat and coat. "They weren't ready for Kenneth at the shelter, and I couldn't leave him; he was in no shape to be left dangling. The guy that runs the place was out of town, and a room that was going to be vacated wasn't. I drove Kenneth around town, until they got a place for him. I would have taken him to the movies, but only horror films were showing." He shrugged. "So."

Anna shook her head. "Poor kid; is he that bad?"

They climbed the stairs. Galen's voice was low. "He's just in a daze. He can answer yes or no—you know, shake his head or nod, but he's just not capable of coherent thinking. He needs a lot of rest, probably hasn't eaten properly in weeks."

"I guess you're too tired to tell me what happened in school," she said.

"We'll talk about it tomorrow."

They undressed and got into bed. Galen sighed and pulled the covers up. Anna reached to turn off the light.

"Oh," she said, "I forgot. You had a phone call."

"Umm," Galen said, his eyes closed.

"About nine–nine-thirty."

"Who?" Galen rolled over.

"Reverend Richter. He said he wanted you to come up to the church basement. He said he needed to talk to you. He sounded funny."

Galen opened his eyes and raised his head. "Do you think I should call him?"

Anna rose and went to the window. "No, it's too late; everything's dark at the parsonage."

Galen's voice was muffled. "I'll see him tomorrow."

Anna climbed into bed, pressed against his back, and kissed his shoulder.

The next morning after breakfast Galen went to the phone. He looked out the window, trying to decide which call to make first. It was a sparkling day, the kind that used to make him think of sucker fishing below Stauffer's Dam. The hills looked inviting too, but there were things to do. Charlie Buch would be calling to ask him to drive the hearse for Grandma Lesher's funeral. And he had to check with Doc. He looked up toward the sexton's cottage as he dialed Doc's number.

The phone rang several times; a woman's voice answered.

"Mrs. Evans, may I talk with Doc? This is Galen Herr."

"I'm sorry, Mr. Herr; the doctor isn't in."

Galen frowned. "Can I reach him by phone?"

"I'm afraid not. He didn't come in last night, and I haven't heard from him yet this morning. Shall I have him call you when he returns?"

"Isn't that unusual?" Galen said. "I mean his not coming in last night."

Her voice was sharp. "It *does* happen. He had a call last night from Reverend Richter. He probably had to take somebody to the hospital—and stayed overnight. He may be back in Fair Hill now making some calls—probably is."

"Well, thank you, Mrs. Evans—and please ask him to call me when he gets back to his office."

He hung up the phone. He dialed Richter's number.

The baritone voice answered on the second ring. "The Reverend Richter speaking."

"This is Galen Herr. I'm sorry I was out when you called last night. Hope nothing's wrong."

Richter laughed. "Wrong? I didn't call you last night."

"You didn't?" Galen said. "Maybe somebody was kidding."

"Maybe your students," Richter said.

"Maybe," Galen said. He stared out the window. "Then—"

"Then what?" the phone said.

"Then you didn't call Doc Evans last night either?"

"No, I didn't call Doc Evans last night. What's going on?"

"I just called Doc's office. His wife answered; she said he wasn't home last night—that you called him, and he didn't come back."

"I'm sure nobody called from here—just a moment—Mary Ann!" Galen could hear Richter's wife answer from another room. "No, nobody called from here, Galen."

"Odd."

"It ties in with something I heard this morning in Kutz's store," Richter said.

"What was that?"

"Jake asked me if I'd heard that Doc Evans ran away, with the nurse, the one from Earltown, the one he had a few months back. I thought it was a joke of some kind."

"It's ridiculous," Galen said. "Doc has a good practice, plans for a nice home. Why should he kick all that down the drain?"

"According to Jake, Doc and the nurse have been having an affair. Phares Zercher told Jake this morning he once caught them parked on Zimmerman's Hill. Jake says he heard Doc's gone to meet her in California." The preacher paused. "Could be. California's a haven for adulterers. You know Doc never came to church."

"Have you seen Phares this morning?"

"No, but he's probably around someplace; he'll have to fill in the grave after Grandma Lesher's funeral."

"O.K., Reverend. I'm glad you didn't need me after all," Galen said.

"No, everything's fine, Galen; thanks for calling."

Galen hung up the phone. He frowned and looked out the window. Someone impersonating Reverend Richter had called him. Probably the same person had called Doc. Doc had answered the call; now, he was nowhere to be found. And today Doc was to order exhumation of the body. Galen sat, tapping his foot. He reached for the telephone directory—*Klein, Koffroth, Kulp. Kulp, Barton.*

A woman's voice answered.

"Hello," Galen said. "Is this the Kulps'?"

"Ja, here iss Kulps."

"Is Suzie there?" Galen said.

"No, do you know where she iss? We're worried sick."

"Was she home last night?"

"No, she wasn't; she had worked at Doc Evans', and she doesn't stay there overnight."

"When did you see her last?"

"She came home for dinner yesterday, but not for supper."

"Do you know what time she left Evans'?"

"Ja, I called Mrs. Evans. It was around six o'clock. . . . We called all the places she works at still. We chust don't know what to make of it. Now, who am I talking to anyway?"

"This is Galen Herr. I thought we could get Suzie to do some housework when she comes in."

Galen hung up. He stared out the window. Had Phares and Suzie run away? But how? In Doc's car? Perhaps they had abducted Doc or got rid of him? Somehow the idea of Phares and Suzie barreling out of Fair Hill in Doc Evans' Olds was comic. He looked at the poplars, bare and shaggy, and at the great oak beyond Jonas' grave still clinging to its dead leathery leaves.

What to do now? Notify the State Police about missing persons? My God, what is all this anyhow? Maybe he should have listened to Richter and let God handle it. Maybe he should have heeded Doc and left everything the way it was.

He looked at the pile of brown earth that would soon cover what was left of Grandma Lesher. The green artificial grass rug would be spread over it so that relatives would be spared the realization of the meaning of "dust to dust." But after the few words, the crowd would leave, the rug would be removed, and the sexton would shovel the dirt in. The sexton—that was Phares—but Phares was a missing person. Who would fill in the hole?

As Galen looked, a figure entered the cemetery. Galen's breath caught. Phares. The bearded giant came nearer. He walked up to the open grave; walked around it, looking in. He kicked a clot of earth into the grave, turned, and walked toward the church. He stopped and looked toward Galen's house.

Galen leaned back into shadow. Christ, he thought, Phares is here. Doc is missing. Suzie is missing. But Phares is here.

If I had answered that phone call last night, where would I be?

He pulled a chair away from the line of the window and sat, limply. Morning coffee bubbled into his throat, and he swallowed.

17

Later he went into the kitchen.

"Let's have a little lunch; you hungry?" Anna said.

"Not really, but I guess I better have something. I have to put on my dark suit."

Anna put the luncheon meat on the table and started to heat soup. By the time Galen got back, lunch was ready. They ate without talking.

"You didn't eat much," Anna said.

"I told you I wasn't hungry." He picked up his dish and placed it in the sink.

She waited. "You seem nervous; did you get enough sleep?"

Galen smiled. "I never drove a hearse before; maybe I'm excited about that." He opened the closet door and took the shoeshine kit from the shelf. Ann stacked her dishes in the sink and cleared the table.

Galen was polishing the second shoe when the phone rang. Anna dried her hands on her apron and lifted the receiver.

"Hello . . . oh, hello, Alma . . . yes, he's here . . . I'm

sure he can, Alma, but let me ask him." Anna held the phone to her breast and spoke to Galen. "Can you go up to Buch's right now?"

Galen frowned. "Sure, I can, I guess. What's the trouble?"

Anna put her hand over the mouthpiece. "Alma seems upset," she said. "She didn't tell me why."

"I can be up in five minutes," Galen said.

"Alma," Anna said into the phone, "he'll be up right away."

Galen put the kit away, and took out his overcoat.

"Galen," Anna said, "didn't I hear you talking to Milt Frey on the phone before lunch?"

"Yes," Galen said.

"What did you want with him?"

"Nothing much," Galen said.

"He's the constable."

"I know he's the constable."

"What did you want with him?"

Galen opened the door. "I want him to be ready to arrest Phares Zercher. I just told him to be at a certain place at a certain time."

"And you're going to be there?"

"Yes," Galen said. "Yes. I think Phares might make a statement."

"Are you crazy?"

Galen came over and kissed her forehead. "I have to go, dear."

"Tell me before you leave," Anna said.

"Tell you what?"

"Tell me, 'Don't worry, honey, everything will be all right.' "

Galen said, "Don't worry, honey, everything will be all right," and closed the door behind him.

The Saturday noon siren wailed as Galen pushed the bell button of Buch's Funeral Home. Alma opened the door immediately.

Her face was pale. "Oh, I'm glad you got here. It's already twelve o'clock."

"What's the matter?" Galen took off his coat. Alma stood by the large open stairway. The draped and carpeted house was silent.

"It's Charlie," she said. Her hands worked at the back of her hair, tucking in the bun. She didn't look at him.

"What's wrong?"

"He's dr . . . he's dru . . ." She faced him. "He's been drinking!"

"Well?" Galen said.

"He got up this morning before daylight—said he couldn't sleep." She sniffed. "He said he was going to work in the preparation room. You know I never bother him when he's down there. About ten-thirty, George came to ask about getting things ready at the graveside. I called down and got no answer. I told George to go ahead and do what had to be done. Then I went down and there was Charlie out cold on the preparation table. An empty whisky bottle was standing near the embalming machine."

"Good night," Galen said. "Where is he now?"

"I worked on him and got him awake; then I got him up to the kitchen; it took about an hour to do that, but he's out there now. But I can't get him upstairs into the shower." She rubbed her white knuckles. "Then I called you. The funeral's in just two hours—we've got to do something!"

Galen walked into the kitchen. It was clean, sparkling with appliances. Charlie sat in a chair, his head resting on the table edge.

"Well, that's encouraging," Galen said.

Alma sniffed. "What's encouraging? I don't see anything so—"

"He's smiling," Galen said. "If he were really drunk, his lips would be hanging and flapping."

"Oh, do something," Alma moaned.

Galen put his hand on Charlie's shoulder. "Hey, Charlie," he said, pulling him up.

Charlie's hands fell from the table into his lap and his head tilted back against the wall. His eyes opened.

"*Charlie* Buch, aren't you ashamed!" Alma said.

Charlie looked at Galen. He lurched to his feet and held out his hand. "Hi, Gale, buddy," he said. His shirt was open, his necktie awry, his hair rumpled. He leaned forward.

Galen took his hand. "Boy, you're drunk. What happened?"

"Why did you do it, Charlie?" Alma cried. "If this ever gets out—"

"He'll be all right, Alma," Galen said. "Do you have instant coffee?" Alma nodded. "Put some water on."

Charlie swayed. "I'm sold cober. Never better shape m'life." He hiccoughed, then giggled.

"One good thing, Alma," Galen said, "you can tell he doesn't do this often."

"Don't defend him. He has the streak in him." She slammed a pot into the sink and turned hot water on full force.

"Don't worry 'bout ol' Charlie. I'm aw right. 'F Reveren' Richter came in—couldn' tell thing."

"There's a funeral today," Alma said. "Did you forget that? Who'd you think was going to bury Grandma Lesher?"

"Don' shu worry 'bout that. We'll get her in," Charlie said.

"Oh!" Alma said.

"You go up to the store," Galen said. "Get a couple packs of mints to kill that breath."

Alma left and Galen began to force-feed the coffee. By the time she returned, Charlie had several cups. The grin was gone from his face.

"Did George take care of things at the grave? Did Weber Electric get the record player back?" Charlie said.

"Everything's all right if you are," Alma said.

"He's looking better every minute," Galen said.

"Maybe if he ate something," Alma said. "Are you hungry?"

Charlie winced. "Maybe a poached egg."

Alma cooked the egg and he ate it tentatively. "Now what time is it?" Charlie asked.

"One—a little after," Galen said.

Charlie felt his face. "I gotta shave. Alma, can you find a black Homburg for Galen? Do you have a black overcoat?" Galen shook his head. "Alma, get Galen a black overcoat, too." He looked at Galen. "Do you think we'll make it?"

"Don't worry," Galen said. "We'll get 'er in."

By quarter of two the guests began to arrive. Alma greeted people with her professional smile. She handed each one a small folded leaflet. On the front was a picture of a church window. Inside, the date of birth and death, and the full name of the deceased and the lines of Tennyson's "Crossing the Bar."

Charlie, pale-faced and red-eyed, shuffled over the thick carpet, shaking hands with members of "the immediate family." Frequently he disappeared into another room to check the record player and to pop another mint onto his dry tongue.

Galen stood in the background and counted the remaining seats. He unfolded and arranged another row of chairs. When Richter began to intone the service, Galen stepped through the double doors at the side. He checked equipment and removed obstacles from the path the pallbearers would take.

He waited outside. He stretched his arms before him and squeezed his hands together, but the kinks in his shoulders held tight. The back of his head ached. He turned his head, pressed his chin against his shoulder, heard muscles creak inside his neck. He sighed and entered the hearse.

The funeral party came outside. Those who had come on foot began walking slowly in the direction of the cemetery. Those who had cars stood in groups until the casket and flowers were placed in the hearse. At the cue from Charlie, Galen started the engine, Milt Frey held up the trickle of Main Street traffic, and the funeral procession began to move.

"You see, Charlie," Galen shifted into second gear, "people think you're so successful you can hire a chauffeur."

Charlie grunted.

They drove for a minute in silence.

"Charlie, listen to me; I need your help," Galen said.

"Speak up," Charlie said. "You ain't gonna disturb Grandma Lesher."

"I want to try something tonight that will wind up this business with Phares Zercher."

"You still at it?"

"Look, we don't have much time. Doc was going to order the exhumation of the body today, but now Doc's missing. That's why I have to do what I plan to do."

"What?"

"I'm going to dig up Jonas' body tonight."

Charlie looked at him. "You're what?"

"At least I'm going to start. If it goes the way I think it will, I won't need to finish. And that's where I need your help."

"Not me," Charlie said. "You don't need my help. You need psychiatric help. I spend days in the cemetery; I don't plan to spend nights there."

"No, no, I don't mean that kind of help. All I want you to do is let Phares know, one way or another, what I mean to do. You'll have plenty of chances. Say it to Richter so that Phares overhears it. Just say, 'Guess what that crazy schoolteacher's gonna do.' "

Charlie shook his head. "I ain't gonna help you get hurt."

"It's safe," Galen said. "I've made arrangements with Milt. I figure if Phares knows I'm down there, he'll try to stop me."

"Damn right."

"Well, Milt's gonna hide behind the oak tree with a rifle. I figure Phares'll say something about why he came to stop me and Milt will hear him and make the arrest. If we have a confession, we won't have to exhume the body."

Galen turned the big Cadillac into the cemetery driveway. The flowers in back rustled.

"You got your mind made up?" Charlie said.

"That's right; if you won't help me, I'll let Phares know some other way." Galen slowed the hearse.

"What time will you do this?" Charlie said. "Not midnight, I hope."

"No—about ten, ten-thirty. Make it ten-thirty, Charlie. I want Milt to have plenty of time to get in position; he's coming in from the ball diamond; I don't want Phares prowling down here too early."

Galen braked the hearse to a stop about fifty feet from the graveside. Many of the people who had walked were already there.

Charlie shrugged. "I'll do it." He hesitated. "But I think I'll call the State Police and get them there too."

Galen shook his head. "And look silly if Phares doesn't bite? Milt'll be all the protection I need. He's a good shot. Call me after supper." Galen climbed out of the car. Charlie went to direct the pallbearers.

18

Framed in the kitchen window, the night was black. Galen looked at his watch—nine-thirty. Milt Frey should be crossing the ball diamond right now. Charlie Buch had called about seven. "Well," he had said, "you've got it. I had a good chance while we were gathering up the stuff. I hope you know what you're doing."

Galen walked to the door.

Anna looked up from her mending. "Where you going?"

"Just out on the porch. I'll be right back." He stood outside and looked at the sky—dark, yet cloudless. *"There's husbandry in heaven; their candles are all out,"* he thought. A slight breeze from the northwest. He shivered and went back into the house.

"You're restless tonight," Anna said.

"It's cold out. Winter's coming."

Anna sewed. "We haven't been out of town together since before Jonas died," she said. "Did you know that?"

"Yeah—we ought to go to Philadelphia soon. Let's plan to do that."

Anna patted her ballooned maternity skirt. "I guess we can't go as long as I'm a prisoner of love."

"We'll soon be liberated," Galen said.

There was silence; Galen looked at his watch again.

"I think I'll go for a little walk, Anna." He got his cap and jacket. Anna looked at him.

"Why don't you sit and talk with me?"

He opened the door. "We'll talk tomorrow; there'll be more to talk about."

"You're going to do something?" she said.

"Don't worry," Galen said.

Outside, he stopped on the walk. Saturday night in Fair Hill. A car squealed around a distant corner. Some kid in Pop's car. Lights were in houses. He heard someone laugh. Charlie's words echoed: "I hope you know what you're doing." The street light shone by Levi Martin's lane. It led down into the valley. Why not take the lane, along the fence rows to the creek, along the crooked creek to Stauffer's Dam, watch the moon on the water? Why not do that? Milt Frey would get tired and take his rifle home. Phares would give up watching the cemetery. And the night would be peaceful and still, and the valley and the water would gleam and whisper under the moon. Phares would tend his business. Jonas would rest. Everyone would go about his own business. Galen Herr would admire the night, and plan a Sunday with his family.

What is Galen Herr's business?

He walked to the tool shed. He took out a pick and a shovel. His students were at the movies, maybe some of them parked on Zimmerman's Hill, maybe at parties, maybe even doing homework. And he was marching through the night to open a grave. He held the pick in his right hand, the shovel in his left, to keep them from clanking.

The graveyard was black. Grass was soft and silent underfoot. Tombstones hulked in the night. Each one Phares crouching. What he saw was still. But movement seemed to flicker always to the side. Galen set his head rigidly.

What was it for? Headlines formed in his head: LOCAL SCHOOLTEACHER MOLESTS GRAVE. FAIR HILL MAN KILLED (shot? choked? stabbed?) IN CEMETERY.

He came to the plot where Jonas lay. He stooped to examine the headstone and to feel the softness of the rectangular mound. About fifty feet away the oak tree loomed, and behind it the small ravine, beyond that, the outfield of the ball diamond.

Galen stood silent. He bumped the shovel against the pick. From behind the oak tree came two short sounds—the kind an insect might make—or a man, sucking air through his upper teeth.

With the pick Galen levered aside one of the stones Phares had laid on the grave. He raised the pick and brought it down sharply. It sank in up to the handle. He swung again. The pick hit a stone. He began to shovel away loose dirt. He dug slowly. He looked and listened as he worked. Sounds echoed from the back wall of the church. Time was endless. The hole grew bigger; Galen worked more slowly, more loudly.

He stopped, stood silent, unwilling to violate more of the grave plot.

"Keep digging, schoolteacher!" The whisper came from behind. Galen froze; his arms tingled and his hands numbed. Phares's voice came again in a tight even rasp. "Keep digging, I said. I got a gun; keep digging or I blow your brains out."

Galen stood.

"Dig, damn you, dig." The voice was closer. Galen jerked the shovel into the ground. Milt was behind the oak tree. Milt was there. He must be there. He realized suddenly that he was standing between the oak tree and the voice.

"Faster."

Galen dug convulsively and stopped.

"Keep digging, God damn it."

Galen tried to move.

"You weak? Dig, you bastard; or I'll kill you right now."

Galen swallowed. "Why do you want me to dig?" His voice was faint.

"I'm going to kill you, schoolteacher; you're the last one."

Galen glanced at the oak tree. "What do you mean, I'm the last one?"

"I must kill until it is clean; you're the last one."

"You're out of your mind, Phares. You don't have to kill anyone. Just"—Galen flushed—"just let me go home."

"No. I have to fix it with Jonas. It's in the Bible. How I make it right again."

"Phares, you're not making sense," Galen said.

"I know what I'm doing. I choked Jonas." His voice shook. "That was a terrible thing."

"Let me go home," Galen said.

"You don't understand nothing. I killed Jonas; now I must make it right. Suzie Kulp—she kept after me. She is evil. I killed her the same way I killed Jonas. *Versteh,* schoolteacher? I killed Doc too—in the basement of the church. He is a bad one. He knew I killed Jonas right from the start—and he didn't care. I know what I should do; I see clearer than I ever did. Now, I'm going to kill you—chust dig the hole a little deeper—and then Jonas will let me sleep and it will be all right."

"Why me?" Galen said.

"Because you wouldn't let me forget what I done; now dig!"

Galen reached for the pick in front of him. Suddenly he fell flat into the shallow hole he had dug. His senses swirled. He burrowed his head into the dirt.

A shot crashed. Galen felt dizzy. He pulled himself on his elbows behind the tombstone. Sound flashed beside the oak tree. Galen fell, his face turned on the dirt. "Am I hit?" he said. "Am I hit?" The earth heaved and turned. "Am I?" he gasped. Then the earth receded and slowed.

He saw, distantly, Phares spin halfway around and drop on

one knee. A siren wailed from somewhere on College Avenue and a pair of headlights approached the back entrance to the cemetery. The porch light came on in Galen's house. Phares began to run among the headstones, hunched low. Milt Frey stepped out from behind the oak tree, levered another shell into the chamber, and fired at the running man.

The car careened up the driveway and slid to a stop below Jonas' plot. Two State Policemen, armed with revolvers, got out quickly. Charlie Buch followed. They ran up to Milt.

"It was Phares Zercher. I think I hit him; he dropped, but then he got up and ran toward the alley." Milt was wearing his hunting clothes. His coat was open and his flannel-shirted belly hung on a sagging belt.

"Where's Galen?" Charlie Buch shouted. The policemen were stabbing the flashlights toward the alley, through the trees, and among the stones.

"He fell," Milt said. "Phares shot." Milt stepped behind Jonas' stone. "He was—here he is, quick."

Charlie ran over and knelt. He lifted Galen's arm from his face. Galen's eyes were closed. In the beam of the flashlight, his flesh was white.

"My God," Charlie said. "Call the ambulance!"

Galen moaned.

"It's all right," Charlie said. "It's all right."

"Aagh," Galen said. "I want to go home. Take me home."

"You lie quiet," Charlie said. "We'll have a doctor here in no time. Where are you hit?"

"Oh-h," Galen said, "I'm not hit. I'm so goddamned scared I can't stand up. I'm scared. I'm scared."

19

Milt Frey leaned over and opened the car door for Galen. Early sun flushed the sky. Galen slid into the passenger seat.

Milt twisted against the wheel. "Galen," he said, "I want you to meet Corporal Ober and Private McGary, of the State Police. They were at the cemetery last night."

The State Troopers sitting in the rear shook hands over the seat back with Galen.

Milt held the gear in neutral. "I don't feel right about this, Galen. We don't need you to find Phares. Something could happen. It's not your job."

Galen sighed. "I wish I knew what my job was. Look, you know he's scared and dangerous. But he confessed to me last night. And maybe now he'll listen to me. Maybe I'm the one he'll listen to. Maybe I can calm him."

Milt shifted into first, his foot on the clutch. "Galen," he said, "are you sure you got the stomach?"

Galen was silent. "I don't blame you for asking," he said. "Can we go on now, please, Milt?"

The car moved from the curb. Galen waved at the house window. Anna, shadowed, made a small gesture.

They rode in silence. Milt turned down the steep dirt road from Silver Hill.

"Are you sure he'll be there?" Corporal Ober said.

"We have to start somewhere," Milt said. "Phares lived at the *Felsakeller* one whole summer. He knows the area."

"It's a good hideout," Ober said. "All those rocks. They say deserters during the Revolutionary War holed up in that cave."

Milt drove through the low rolling woodland and up a dirt road running along the turnpike.

"What's *Felsakeller* mean?" Private McGary said.

"Rock Cellar," Milt said. He drove off the road and parked. "We'll get out here."

They stood outside. Trucks and automobiles whisked by on the nearby dual highway.

"*Did* he kill Suzie Kulp and Doc?" Galen said.

"Well," Milt said, "so far we have only his word. There is no evidence in the church or in Jonas' house. No bloodstains. Nothing."

"No bodies?" Galen said.

"Boy, we searched. No bodies."

"Where we going?" Private McGary said.

Milt pointed across the turnpike. "That's Yellow Hill, caves all among the rocks. There's one big cave Phares would know. Old-timers call it *Diewel's Loch.*"

They followed Milt down the road. McGary shook his head. "Now what the hell does *that* mean?"

Milt laughed. "Devil's Hole."

"How we gonna cross the turnpike?" Corporal Ober said.

Milt tilted the Winchester down under his arm. "Come on," he said. "There's a big drainage tunnel goes under the highway."

The two troopers followed Milt and Galen down the rocky slope. The round tunnel, about ten feet in diameter, was made of corrugated metal sheets. Water trickled along the bottom. Water marks showed six to seven feet high along the sides.

"All we need is a flash flood now," Ober said, his voice hollow and echoing.

Milt stopped, clamped his Winchester under his arm, and pulled a pistol from his jacket pocket.

"Here, Galen," he said.

"Keep it," Galen said. "Keep it."

The sound of turnpike traffic was shut out, except for an occasional grumbled echoing from the rocks at either end. A strong draft, several degrees colder than outside, sucked through the opening in front of them. In places large rocks had washed in, and piles of silt had built up where the stream deflected. Moss, algae, and lichen grew dankly on the sides.

"If he walked—and it looks like he had to—" McGary said, "he had to cross the turnpike—that is, if he's in these hills. We might look for tracks."

"I've been looking," Milt said. "Hunters use this too much for tracks to show anything. But if Phares is on Yellow Hill, he came through here."

They stopped by a large flat rock. The mud around the base was a jumble of footprints. Ober walked around looking at the base. He reached down, picked up a wet rag. He held it by the tip of thumb and forefinger.

"Is this blood?"

Milt took it and examined it. "It's a red bandanna. But this moisture is caking. It may *be* blood. A lot of people use these red handkerchiefs, but if it's blood—"

"It looks fresh," McGary said. "Some of it hasn't caked."

"Layin' in that wet mud, it would stay moist a long time."

"Let's go," Ober said. They emerged on the other side into sunlight, brilliant after the darkness of the tunnel.

"We go straight up," Milt said, pointing. "Just follow the stream; then a trail breaks off to the right."

"We better fan out a little," Ober said.

"Galen, you keep with me," Milt said.

They made their way up slowly into the trees. About three hundred feet up, Galen looked back to the tiny cars flashing below on the turnpike.

They moved along, watching. A grouse flew up. Each man wheeled into the sound and then looked at the others. They came to the rocks—at first small and widely separated, then larger and closer together. The rocks were piled one on top of the other, about the size of freight cars. Trees grew in the spaces between the rocks, and even, in the distance, out of the rocks themselves.

Milt Frey stopped and beckoned. The State Policemen came up and they stood together in a niche between two rocks.

"That hole, like an upside-down V near the top." Milt pointed. "That's the Devil's Hole. If he's in there, he's got a gun; we'll have problems."

"Hell of a way to spend Sunday morning," McGary said.

"Get down," Ober said. They crouched behind the rocks. "I thought I saw something move."

"So did I," McGary said.

They crouched, waiting. Nothing happened.

Milt raised his head. He brought it down quickly and sat, his back against the huge rock. He took off his cap and looked at the others.

"He's there," Milt said.

Ober pulled open the flap of his holster. He clicked the chamber of his revolver to turn a live cartridge into the barrel.

"No," Galen said. "Let me."

Milt shrugged. He levered a cartridge into his rifle. McGary had his revolver in his hand.

"Phares!" Galen shouted.

Milt waved Corporal Ober and Private McGary out. The troopers began to crawl among the rocks.

"Phares!" Galen said.

The voice came down, harsh and strong. "Schoolteacher?"

"Phares," Galen said. "Come back with us. We can help you. Come back with us."

"I don't need no help." A rock skittered down.

Milt looked around the side. "He's standing just inside the cave."

"Phares," Galen cried, "Kenneth needs you. Whatever is done, we can help you."

"Kenneth." The voice was thin. "I know what Kenneth needs. I know."

About two hundred feet west and fifty feet lower, Ober waved gently to Milt.

"Galen," Milt said, "we've got the crossfire now." He rolled over and laid the rifle along the rockside. He lay flat, sighting.

"Phares!" Galen said.

Phares stepped out from the cave. "I got what is needed, schoolteacher," he shouted. The black thing in his massive hand swung up before him.

A shot crashed from below and Phares staggered. He tried to swing the black object up before him again.

Galen leaped up and ran toward the line of fire from below. "No!" Galen screamed. "No. He has no gun!"

Phares turned and held the black thing straight out toward Galen. The giant thrust himself forward. Galen leaped up on a rock in the way. Phares stumbled forward, his arm up in the air. It settled down, pointed rigidly at Galen, the great hand clenched on the object. "Schoolteacher!" he cried. "In the grave!"

Galen leaped. A shot crashed and a blow on the hip whirled Galen in mid-air. Milt's rifle snapped and Phares fell straight forward, almost on top of Galen.

Fire filled Galen's hip. "It's a Bible," he whimpered. "It's a Bible. God damn it, it's a Bible!"

20

Galen woke, flat on his back. Rearing before him was the great white column of his leg, suspended from an overhead hoist.

"Galen?" Anna said.

"Oh," Galen said. "Anna."

She moved to the bedside. "Darling," she said, "you're all right."

"I can't feel anything, Anna."

She turned sidewise, her hand on the large-bellied skirt, and sat gently on the bedside. "Darling," she said, "they gave you drugs. It'll be all right."

Galen swallowed. "My hip?"

"It'll be all right, dear. It'll be all right."

"Will I be able—?"

Anna smiled, her eyes glistening. "It'll be all right, dear."

"I know," Galen said. "Don't worry?"

Anna rose. "Reverend Richter and Charlie Buch are outside. Shall I send them in?" Her face was turned away. Her voice was strong.

Galen closed his eyes. "I don't care."

The door closed.

Galen lay, not moving.

The door opened.

Galen watched Charlie Buch, a rolled newspaper in his hand, and the Reverend Richter, a Bible clasped in both hands, come in.

A nurse stood framed in the doorway. "Five minutes, gentlemen," she said.

"Boy," Charlie Buch said, "I'm glad to see you." He cleared his throat. "I'm glad to see you." He unrolled the newspaper and said loudly, "You're a hero! Look, Galen, you're a genuine hero."

"Yes," Galen said.

Charlie looked at him and rolled up the newspaper.

"Praise be to God," Richter said. "We rejoice that you have been spared, Galen."

"Are you going to bury Phares?" Galen said.

"Yes, I am," Richter said. "Although some of the congregation think it wrong, I will conduct the services over Phares Zercher. For his, too, is a soul that—"

"Yes," Galen said.

"Listen," Charlie said. "Wait till you hear. They found Doc and Suzie!"

"Alive?" Galen whispered. "Alive?"

"Oh, no," Charlie said. "Milt figured it out. Milt had us dig Grandma Lesher up again. Phares was a real fox, boy. The night he killed Doc and Suzie, he dug the open grave a little deeper, drug them out of the church and his house, I guess, and buried them right in that grave. Milt said Phares gave him the idea. Phares yelled, 'In the grave,' Milt said."

"Suzie and Doc are dead," Galen said.

"We opened the grave today; the bodies were there. Just three inches below the bottom surface. Boy, we never dreamed we were putting Grandma Lesher on top of Doc and Suzie, did we?"

Galen turned his head.

The Reverend Richter lifted his clasped hands. "We better go, Charlie. Galen is tiring." The preacher bent his head.

"Our heavenly Father," he said.

Charlie bowed his head.

"We are grateful," Richter said, "to Thee that in Thy great mercy Thou didst spare the life of this Thy servant, our beloved brother. Grant Thou, most merciful heavenly Father, that he may be sustained through the remaining days of his convalescence and speedily strengthened in mind and body so that he may return to his loved ones and to Thy continued service, Amen."

Galen watched Charlie Buch and the Reverend Richter go to the door.

Charlie stopped. "Galen," he said, "Phares had that old German Bible with him."

"Yes," Galen said. "I know."

"I guess," Charlie said, "he was getting rid of his sins."

"Yes," Galen said. He lifted his head on the pillow. "It's my turn. Now."